Praise for *USA TODAY* bestselling author Marie Ferrarella

"Ferrarella delivers a fabulous couple. Wonderful storytelling expertly delivers both lighthearted and tragic story details."
—*RT Book Reviews* on *Her Red-Carpet Romance*

"An easy-read modern romance with a creditable and self-possessed heroine to steal your heart."
—*Fresh Fiction* on *Mendoza's Secret Fortune*

"She has a genuine knack for keeping the reader interested and involved in the characters and their emotional feelings."
—*Fresh Fiction* on *His Forever Valentine*

"Expert storytelling moves the book along at a steady pace. A solidly crafted plot makes it quite entertaining."
—*RT Book Reviews* on *Cavanaugh Fortune*

"Master storyteller Ferrarella has a magical way of spinning feel-good romances that readers can lose themselves in, and her latest is no exception."
—*RT Book Reviews* on *The Cowboy and the Lady*

Dearest Reader,

Welcome back to the world of the Matchmaking Mamas. This story is in essence about two lost souls, both good people, but both somewhat damaged in the eyes of the world around them. We have Dr. Mitch Stewart, an above-par general surgeon who, while very skilled in his field (and trust me, you want a good doctor, not a conversationalist, when you really, really need one), has absolutely no bedside manner to speak of. Nor does he even realize this is something that is necessary to make him a complete package, both as a person and as a surgeon.

Then there is Melanie McAdams, an elementary teacher on hold. She has taken a leave of absence from her position to volunteer full-time at a shelter in an effort to try to heal her broken heart. Her high school sweetheart, the man she was set to marry, was killed overseas just four days short of returning home to her. Unlike Mitch, she can love, but *won't* love, because the price is too high. These two meet at the homeless shelter where Melanie volunteers and which specializes in single moms with children. It is while helping these lost, displaced people that Mitch and Melanie are brought together by a bright little girl named April who has lost everything. Quite against their intentions, these two accidentally fall in love.

Please, stick around and see how they come to grips with and deal with that little surprise.

As always, I thank you for taking the time to read one of my books and from the bottom of my heart, I wish you someone to love who loves you back.

Marie Ferrarella

Dr. Forget-Me-Not

Marie Ferrarella

Recycling programs
for this product may
not exist in your area

ISBN-13: 978-0-373-65938-8

Dr. Forget-Me-Not

Printed in U.S.A.

USA TODAY bestselling and RITA® Award–winning author **Marie Ferrarella** has written more than two hundred and fifty books for Harlequin, some under the name Marie Nicole. Her romances are beloved by fans worldwide. Visit her website, marieferrarella.com.

Books by Marie Ferrarella

Harlequin Special Edition

Matchmaking Mamas

Coming Home for Christmas
Her Red-Carpet Romance
Diamond in the Ruff
Dating for Two
Wish Upon a Matchmaker
Ten Years Later...
A Perfectly Imperfect Match
Once Upon a Matchmaker

The Fortunes of Texas: Cowboy Country

Mendoza's Secret Fortune

The Fortunes of Texas: Welcome to Horseback Hollow

Lassoed by Fortune

The Fortunes of Texas: Southern Invasion

A Small Fortune

Montana Mavericks: Back in the Saddle

Real Vintage Maverick

Visit the Author Profile page
at Harlequin.com for more titles.

To
Nancy Parodi Neubert,
And
Friendships
That go back to the
3rd Grade

Prologue

"You haven't finally decided to sell that beautiful house of yours and downsize to something a little smaller and more modern, now have you?"

It wasn't really a question. Maizie Connors, sitting opposite the attractive woman in Jack's Hideaway, Bedford's newest trendy restaurant, knew better than to think that Charlotte, a woman she had known for close to forty years, would ever sell the house she loved so much. When she'd taken the unexpected call from her old friend that morning, Maizie had suspected something was up, but she'd instinctively known it had nothing to do with Charlotte making use of Maizie's successful real estate business.

"What?" Charlotte asked. Sitting ramrod straight, doing her best to appear cheerful, Charlotte Stewart was caught off guard by the question. She also felt somewhat embarrassed, not just because of the deception she'd allowed to continue, but because of the real reason for her getting in contact with Maizie in the first place. She cleared her throat and stalled for time. Trying to get her thoughts together in order to find the right words. So far, they had frustratingly managed to elude her. "Oh, no, I haven't," she confessed, then added in a sincere moment of truth, "I don't think I'll ever sell that house. It's where all the good memories are."

Maizie smiled, nodding her head knowingly. Unlike Charlotte, who had gone stylishly gray, Maizie's short bob was a light golden blond, the same color it had been when she'd first met her late husband all those years ago.

"I didn't think so. So, Charlotte," she asked, getting comfortable, "what's this lunch *really* about?"

To be honest, Maizie was fairly certain she knew the answer to her question. As a successful Realtor, she had started her agency after her husband passed away years ago. It did a brisk business; but these days, she was just as accustomed to getting calls from people who sought her services for the business that she ran on the side as she was from people who wanted to either buy or sell houses.

Maizie, along with her two lifelong best friends, had an aptitude for making matches.

Lasting matches.

When Charlotte called, asking to see her over lunch, the woman had murmured something about needing advice and alluded to it being about selling her house. Surprised—since Maizie knew how attached her friend was to the only place she had ever called home once Charlotte's late husband had slipped a ring on her finger, Maizie had played along until after appetizers had been ordered.

When Charlotte now made no reply to her question, Maizie leaned forward over the small table and placed her hand over her friend's.

"We've been friends for almost forty years, Charlotte, you can tell me. No matter what it is, at my age, I've heard it before."

Charlotte continued to look uncomfortable. "I don't know where to start."

Maizie's smile was warm, encouraging. "Just jump right in and I'll try to keep up."

"It's Mitchell," Charlotte finally blurted out, referring to her only child.

Again, Maizie was fairly certain she knew what was coming, but she approached the subject slowly, not wanting to make her friend nervous enough to abruptly change her mind and table the subject.

Guessing at the true reason for this impromptu meeting, Maizie was well aware that the subject the other woman was attempting to broach was not an easy one for some mothers. Although genuinely concerned, mothers like Charlotte didn't want to be seen as meddling, which was only a cut above words like *controlling*, *calculating* and *interfering*. No true mother wanted that label.

"Ah, how is Dr. Mitch these days?" Maizie asked, her blue eyes sparkling with humor.

The word escaped Charlotte's lips before she could think to prevent it. "Lonely."

"Is he?" Maizie asked with keen interest. She loved matching up people with their dream homes.

She loved matching people up with their dream soul mates even more. The former came with a commission, the latter was priceless to her, even if the service itself was free.

"Except he doesn't know it yet," Charlotte hurriedly qualified.

Maizie was nothing if not patience personified. "Explain," she requested.

"He'd really be annoyed if he knew I was saying this," Charlotte interjected hesitantly.

"Then we won't tell him," Maizie assured her pleasantly. None of the protagonists in the matches she and her friends had undertaken ever knew that their "meetings" had been orchestrated. Things worked out far more naturally that way. "But you're going to have to give me a little more to work with here."

Charlotte took a deep breath and forged ahead, knowing that if she lost her nerve, if she told Maizie "never mind" and just left, the problem would only continue. And most likely get worse. She loved her son far too much to let that happen. He deserved to have a full life.

"Mitchell is a fantastic surgeon," she said by way of an introduction to the crux of the matter.

Maizie nodded. "Like his father." She was rewarded with a grateful smile from her friend.

"But he lacks Matthew's gift for getting along with people." Charlotte hesitated for a moment, knowing that wasn't specific enough. She tried again. "He just doesn't *connect*."

"With his patients?" Maizie asked, quietly urging her friend on. She vaguely remembered Charlotte's son as a quiet, intense young man.

"With anybody." Charlotte sighed as she leaned forward over the table toward Maizie. "He's brilliant, handsome and you couldn't ask for a better surgeon— or a better son," she tacked on.

"But...?" Maizie asked, fully aware that the word was waiting in the wings.

"But I'm never going to have any grandchildren." Charlotte appeared distressed at the words she had just blurted out. "I know it sounds trivial—"

Maizie quickly cut her off. "Trust me, I understand perfectly. I was in your shoes once. So were some of my friends. Sometimes, you can't just sit back and wait for the planets to align themselves. Sometimes, you have to drag those planets into place yourself," Maizie told her with a wink. And then Maizie got down to business. "As far as you know, has Mitchell ever been seriously involved with anyone?"

"I *do* know." Charlotte prided herself on the fact that she had the kind of relationship with Mitch where her son actually *talked* to her. "And he hasn't. I once watched a young woman all but throw herself at him at a party—it was a fund raiser for his hospital," she interjected. "Anyway, Mitchell had absolutely no idea that she was doing it." Charlotte pressed her lips together as she shook her head, recalling the incident. "I'm beginning to think things are hopeless."

Maizie was always at her best when faced with a challenge. A string of successes had only bolstered her confidence in her knack—as well as Celia's and Theresa's—for bringing the right people together.

"Never hopeless," Maizie assured her. "Let me ask around and see what I can do." She patted Charlotte's hand and repeated, "Never hopeless." And then she grinned. "Now we can order," she declared since her agenda had come into focus. "I don't know about you, Charlotte, but I'm suddenly starved."

Chapter One

She was doing her best to get lost in other people's lives.

Melanie McAdams knew she should be grateful for the fact that she was in a position to help them—which was what she was doing here at the Bedford Rescue Mission, a homeless shelter where single mothers could come with their children and remain as long as needed. The women were encouraged to attempt to stitch together a better life for themselves and their children. Melanie had been volunteering here for almost three years now—and when, nine months ago, her own life had suddenly fallen apart, she'd taken a leave from her job and volunteered at the shelter full-time.

But today, nothing seemed to be working. Today, trying to make a difference in these people's lives wasn't enough to keep the dark thoughts from the past from infiltrating her mind and haunting her.

Because today was nine months to the day when the somber black car had come down her street and stopped in front of her house—the house she and Jeremy had planned to share. Nine months to the day when she'd opened her front door to find a chaplain and army lieutenant John Walters standing on her doorstep, coming to solemnly tell her that her whole world had just been blown up.

Coming to tell her that Jeremy Williams, her high school sweetheart, her fiancé, her *world*, wasn't coming back to her.

Ever.

No matter how good she was, no matter how hard she prayed, he wasn't coming back.

Except in a coffin.

Melanie gave up trying to stack the children's books on the side table in one of the shelter's two common rooms. They just kept sliding and falling on the floor.

When did it stop? Melanie silently demanded. When did it stop hurting like this? When did the pain fade into the background instead of being the first thing she was aware of every morning and the last thing that she was aware of every night? When did it stop chewing bits and pieces out of her every day?

Four days, she thought now. Four days, that was how long Jeremy had had left. Four days and he would have been out of harm's way once and for all. His tour of duty would have been over.

Four days and he would have been back in her arms, back in her life, taking vows and marrying her.

But it might as well have been four hundred years. It hadn't happened.

Wasn't going to happen.

Because Jeremy was now in a cold grave instead of her warm bed.

"Are you okay, Miss Melody?" the small, high-pitched voice asked.

Trying to collect herself as best she could, Melanie turned around to look down into the face of the little girl who had asked the question. The small, concerned face and older-than-her-years green eyes belonged to April O'Neill, a beautiful, bright five-year-old who, along with her seven-year-old brother, Jimmy, and her mother, Brenda, had been here at the shelter for a little over a month. Prior to that, they had been living on the streets in a nearby city for longer than their mother had been willing to admit.

Initially, when April had first made the mistake and called her Melody, Melanie had made an attempt to correct her. But after three more attempts, all without success, she'd given up.

She'd grown to like the name April called her and had more than a little affection for the small family who had been through so much through no real fault of their own. It was an all too familiar story. A widow, Brenda had lost her job and, after failing to pay the rent for two months, she and her children had been evicted.

With no husband in the picture and no family anywhere to speak of, the street became their home until a police officer took pity on them, loaded them into the back of his squad car and drove them over to the shelter.

Melanie told herself to focus on their problems and the problems of the other homeless women and single mothers who were under the shelter's roof. Their situations were fixable, hers was not.

Melanie forced herself to smile at April. "I'm fine, honey."

April appeared unconvinced. Her small face puckered up, as if she was trying to reconcile two different thoughts. "But your eye is leaking, like Mama's does sometimes when she's thinking sad thoughts, or about Daddy."

"Dust," Melanie told her, saying the first thing that occurred to her. "There's dust in the air and I've got allergies. It makes my eyes...leak sometimes," she said, using April's word for it and hoping that would be enough for the little girl.

April was sharper than she'd been at her age, Melanie discovered.

"Oh. You can take a pill," the little girl advised her. "The lady on TV says you can take a pill to make your all-er-gee go away," she concluded solemnly, carefully pronouncing the all-important word.

April made her smile despite the heaviness she felt on her chest. Melanie slipped her arm around the very small shoulders, giving the little girl a quick hug.

"I'll have to try that," she promised. "Now, why did you come looking for me?" she asked, diverting the conversation away from her and back to April.

April's expression became even more solemn as she stated the reason for her search. "Mama says that Jimmy's sick again."

Melanie did a quick calculation in her head. That made three times in the past six weeks. There was no doubt about it. Jimmy O'Neill was a sickly boy. His time on the street had done nothing to improve that.

"Same thing?" she asked April.

The blond head bobbed up and down with alacrity. "He's coughing and sneezing and Mama says he shouldn't be around other kids or they'll get sick, too."

"Smart lady," Melanie agreed.

As she started to walk to the communal quarters that the women and their children all shared, April slipped her hand through hers. The small fingers tightened around hers as if she was silently taking on the role of guide despite the fact that she and her family had only been at the shelter a short time.

"I think Jimmy needs a doctor," April confided, her eyes meeting Melanie's.

"Even smarter lady," Melanie commented under her breath.

The comment might have been quiet, but April had heard her and went on talking as if they were two equals, having a conversation. "But we don't have any money and Jimmy feels too sick to go to the hospital place. Besides, Mama doesn't like asking for free stuff," April confided solemnly.

Melanie nodded. "Your mama's got pride," she told the little girl. "But sometimes, people have to forget about their pride if it means trying to help someone they love."

April eyed her knowingly. "You mean like Jimmy?"

"Exactly like Jimmy."

Turning a corner, she pushed open the oversize door that led into one of the three large communal rooms that accommodated as many families as could be fit into it without violating any of the fire department's safety regulations. Polly, the woman who ran the shelter, referred to the rooms as dorms, attempting to create a more positive image for the women who found themselves staying here.

The room that April had brought her to was largely empty except for the very worried-looking, small, dark-haired woman sitting on the bed all the way over in the corner. The object of her concern was the rather fragile-looking red-haired little boy sitting up and leaning against her.

The boy was coughing. It was the kind of cough that fed on itself, growing a little worse with each pass and giving no sign of letting up unless some kind of action was taken. Sometimes, it took something as minor as a drink of water to alleviate the cough, other times, prescription cough medicine was called for.

Melanie gave the simplest remedy a try first.

Looking down at the little girl who was still holding her hand, she said, "April, why don't you go to the kitchen and ask Miss Theresa to give you a glass of water for your brother?"

April, eager to help, uncoupled herself from Melanie's hand and immediately ran off to the kitchen.

As April took off, Melanie turned her attention to Jimmy's mother. "He really should see a doctor," she gently suggested.

Worn and tired way beyond her years, Brenda O'Neill raised her head proudly and replied, "We'll manage, thank you. It's not the first time he's had this cough and it won't be the last," she said with assurance. "It comes and goes. Some children are like that."

"True," Melanie agreed. She wasn't here to argue, just to comfort. "But it would be better if it went—

permanently." She knew the woman was proud, but she'd meant what she'd said to April. Sometimes pride needed to take a backseat to doing what was best for someone you loved. "Look, I know that money's a problem, Brenda." She thought of the newly erected, state-of-the-art hospital that was less than seven miles away from the shelter. "I'll pay for the visit."

The expression on Jimmy's mother's face was defiant and Melanie could see the woman withdrawing and closing herself off.

"He'll be all right," Brenda insisted. "Kids get sick all the time."

Melanie sighed. She couldn't exactly kidnap the boy and whisk him off to the ER, not without his mother's express consent. "Can't argue with that," Melanie agreed.

"I brought water," April announced, returning. "And Miss Theresa, too." She glanced over her shoulder as if to make sure that the woman was still behind her. "She was afraid I'd spill it, but I wouldn't," she told Melanie in what the little girl thought passed for a whisper. It didn't.

Theresa Manetti gave the glass of water to Jimmy. "There you go. Maybe this'll help." She smiled at the boy. "And if it doesn't, I might have something else that will."

Brenda looked at the older woman and she squared her shoulders. "I've already had this discussion with that lady," she waved her hand at Melanie. "We can't afford a doctor. Jimmy'll be fine in a couple of days," she insisted, perhaps just a little too strongly, as if trying to convince herself as well as the women she was talking to.

Theresa nodded. A mother of two herself, she fully sympathized with what Jimmy's mother was going through. But she didn't volunteer her time, her crew and the meals she personally prepared before coming here just to stand idly by if there was something she could do. Luckily, after her conversation with Maizie yesterday, there was. It was also, hopefully, killing two birds with one stone—or, as she preferred thinking of it, spreading as much good as possible.

"Good to know, dear," she said to Brenda, patting the woman's shoulder. "But maybe you might want to have Dr. Mitch take a look at him anyway."

"Dr. Mitch?" Melanie asked. This was the first reference she'd heard to that name. Was the volunteer chef referring to a personal physician she intended to call?

"Sorry, that's what my friend calls him," Theresa apologized. "His full name is Dr. Mitchell Stewart and he's a general surgeon associated with Bedford Memorial Hospital—right down the road," she added for Brenda's benefit. "He's been doing rather well these past couple of years and according to mutual sources, he wants to give a little back to the community. When I told Polly about it," she said, referring to Polly French, the director of the shelter, "she immediately placed a call to his office and asked him to volunteer a few hours here whenever he could." She moved aside the hair that was hanging in April's eyes, fondly remembering when she used to do the same thing with her own daughter. "He'll be here tomorrow. I'm spreading the word."

Brenda still looked somewhat suspicious of the whole thing. "We don't need any charity."

"Seems to me that it'll be you being charitable to him," Theresa pointed out diplomatically. "If the man wants to do something good, I say let him." Theresa turned her attention to Jimmy who had mercifully stopped coughing, at least for now. "What about you, Jimmy? What d'you say?"

Jimmy looked up at her with hesitant, watery eyes. "He won't stick me with a needle, will he?"

"I don't think he's planning on that," Theresa replied honestly. "He just wants to do what's best for you."

"Then okay," the boy replied, then qualified one more time, "as long as he doesn't stick me."

Theresa smiled at Brenda. "Born negotiator, that one. Sounds a lot like my son did at that age. He's a lawyer now," Theresa added proudly. "Who knows, yours might become one, too."

The hopeless look on Brenda's face said she didn't agree, but wasn't up to arguing the point.

Theresa gently squeezed the woman's shoulder. "It'll get better, dear. Even when you feel like you've hit bottom and there's no way back up to the surface, it'll get better," Theresa promised.

For her part, Theresa was remembering how she'd felt when her husband had died suddenly of a heart attack. At first, she had been convinced that she couldn't even go on breathing—but she had. She not only went on breathing, but she'd gone on to form and run a successful catering business. Life was nothing if not full of possibilities—as long as you left yourself open to them, Theresa thought.

The last part of her sentence was directed more

toward Melanie than to the young mother she was initially addressing.

"I'd better get back to getting dinner set up," Theresa said, beginning to walk away.

Melanie followed in her wake. "Are you really getting a doctor to come to the shelter?" she asked.

It was hard for her to believe and harder for her to contain her excitement. This was just what some of the children—not to mention some of the women— needed, to be examined by a real doctor.

"Not me, personally," she told Melanie, "but I have a friend who has a friend—the upshot is, yes, there is a doctor coming here tomorrow."

"Photo op?" Melanie guessed. This was the Golden State and a lot of things were done here for more than a straightforward reason. It seemed like everyone thrived on publicity for one reason or another. "Don't get me wrong," she said quickly, "some of these people really need to be seen by a doctor, but if this is just some kind of publicity stunt so that some doctor can drum up goodwill and get people to come to his state-of-the-art new clinic, or buy his new skin cream, or whatever, I don't want to see Brenda and her son being used."

Sympathy flooded Theresa's eyes. She had to restrain herself to keep from hugging Melanie. "Oh honey, what happened to you to make you so suspicious and defensive?"

She was *not* about to talk about Jeremy, or any other part of her life. Besides, that had nothing to do with this.

"This isn't about me," Melanie retorted, then caught hold of her temper. This wasn't like her. She was going to have watch that. "This is about them." She waved her hand toward where they had left Brenda and her children. "I don't want them being used."

"They won't be," Theresa assured her kindly. "This doctor really does see the need to give back a little to the community." That was the story Maizie and the doctor's mother, Charlotte, had told her they'd agreed upon. "He's a very decent sort," she added.

Melanie looked at her, confused. "I thought you said you didn't know him."

"I don't," Theresa readily admitted. "But I know the woman who knows his mother and Maizie would never recommend anyone—even a doctor—who was just out for himself." Theresa paused for a moment as little things began to fall into place in her mind. She had the perfect approach, she thought suddenly, pleased with herself.

"Dr. Mitch is a little...*stiff*, I hear, for lack of a better word. I hate to ask, but maybe you can stick around a little longer, act as a guide his first day here. Show him the ropes."

Melanie would have thought that Polly, the director who was bringing him on board, would be much better suited for the job than she was. "I don't know anything about medicine."

"No, but you know people," Theresa was quick to point out, playing up Melanie's strengths, "and the ones around here seem to trust you a lot."

Melanie shrugged. She didn't know if that was exactly accurate. She was just a familiar face for them. "They're just desperate..." she allowed, not wanting to take any undue credit.

Theresa laughed, nodding. "Aren't we all, one way or another?" This was the perfect point to just retreat, before Melanie could think of any further objections to her interacting with Mitch on a one-to-one basis. So Theresa did. "I really do need to get back to the kitchen to get things set up and ready or dinner is going to be late," she told Melanie.

About to leave, Theresa hesitated. It wasn't just small sad faces that got to her. She'd been infinitely aware of the sadness in Melanie's eyes from the first moment she'd been introduced to the volunteer.

Coming closer to Melanie, she lowered her voice so that only Melanie could hear her. "But I just wanted to tell you that should you ever need to talk—or maybe just need a friendly ear—I'm here at the shelter every other week." She knew she was telling Melanie something that she already knew. "And when I'm not—"

Digging into the pocket of her apron, Theresa extracted one of her business cards. Taking a pen out of the other pocket, she quickly wrote something on the back of the card, then held the same card out to Melanie.

"Here."

Melanie glanced at the front of the card. "Thank you, but I don't think I'm going to be having any parties that'll need catering any time soon."

Theresa didn't bother wasting time telling the young woman that she wasn't offering her catering service, but her services as a sympathetic listener. "That's my private number on the back. If I'm not home, leave a message."

Melanie didn't believe in pouring out her heart and burdening people, especially if they were all but strangers. "But we don't really know each other," she protested, looking at the card.

"That's what phone calls are for," Theresa told her. "To change that." She paused for a moment, as if debating whether or not to say something further. "I know what it feels like to lose someone you love."

Melanie stared at her, stunned. She'd exchanged a few words with the other woman and found Theresa Manetti to be a very sweet person, but she'd never shared anything remotely personal with her, and certainly not the fact that her fiancé had been killed. Why was the woman saying this to her?

As if reading her mind, Theresa told her, "The director told me about your young man. I am very, very sorry."

Melanie stiffened slightly. "Yes, well, I am, too," she replied, virtually shutting down.

But Theresa wasn't put off so quickly. "I think it's a very good thing, your being here. The best way to work through what you're feeling right now is to keep busy, very, very busy. You have to stay ahead of the pain until you can handle it and it won't just mow you down."

"I am never going to be able to handle it," Melanie told her with finality.

"I think you're underestimating yourself," she told Melanie. "You're already thinking of others. Trying to talk that young mother into taking her son to see a doctor is definitely thinking of others."

Melanie's mouth dropped open. She stared at the older woman. "How did you know?" She'd had that conversation with Brenda before Theresa had come on the scene.

Theresa merely smiled, approximating, she knew, the look that sometimes crossed Maizie's face. She swore that she and Celia were becoming more like Maizie every day. "I have my ways, dear," she told Melanie just before leaving. "I have my ways."

Chapter Two

He was having second thoughts.

Serious second thoughts.

Anyone who was vaguely acquainted with Dr. Mitchell Stewart knew him to be focused, dedicated, exceedingly good at everything he set out to do and definitely not someone who could even remotely be conceived of as being impetuous. The latter meant that having second thoughts was not part of his makeup.

Ever.

However, in this one singular instance, Mitch was beginning to have doubts about the wisdom of what he had agreed to undertake.

It didn't mean that he wasn't up to it because he lacked the medical savvy. What he would be doing amounted to practicing random medicine, something he hadn't really done since his intern days. These days he was an exceptionally skilled general surgeon who garnered the admiration and praise of his colleagues as well as the head of his department and several members of his hospital's board of directors.

Mitch could truthfully say that he had never been challenged by any procedure he'd had to perform. In the arena of the operating world, it was a given that he shined—each and every time. He made sure of it, and was dedicated to continuing to make that an ongoing fact of his life.

But just as he knew his strengths, Mitch was aware of the area where he did *not* shine. While he was deemed to be a poetic virtuoso with a scalpel, when it came to words, to expressing his thoughts and explaining what he was going to do to any layman, he was sadly lacking in the proper skills and he was aware of that.

However, that was not enough for him to attempt to change anything that he did, or even to attempt to learn how to communicate better than he did. He didn't have time for that.

Mitch truly felt that successfully operating on an at-risk patient far outweighed making said patient feel better verbally about what was about to happen. His awareness of his shortcoming was, however, just enough for him to acknowledge that this was an area in which he was sorely lacking.

Hence, the second thoughts.

As he drove to the Bedford Rescue Mission now, Mitch readily admitted to himself that he'd agreed to volunteer his services at the local homeless shelter in a moment of general weakness. His mother had ambushed him unexpectedly, showing up on his doorstep last Sunday to remind him that it was his birthday and that she was taking him out to lunch whether he liked it or not.

She had assumed that as with everything else that didn't involve his operating skills, he had forgotten about his birthday.

He had.

But, in his defense, he'd pointed out to her patiently, he'd stopped thinking of birthdays as something to celebrate around the time he'd turned eighteen. That was the year that his father had died and immediately after that, he'd had to hustle, utilizing every spare moment he had to earn money in order to pay his way through medical school.

Oh, there had been scholarships, but they didn't cover everything at the school he had elected to attend and he was not about to emerge out of medical school with a degree and owing enough money, thanks to student loans, to feed and clothe the people of a small developing nation for a decade. If emerging debt free meant neglecting everything but his work and his studies, so be it.

Somewhere along the line, holidays and birthdays had fallen by the wayside, as well. His life had been stripped down to the bare minimum.

But he couldn't strip away his mother that easily. He loved her a great deal even if he didn't say as much. The trouble was his mother was dogged about certain things, insisting that he at least spend time with her on these few occasions, if not more frequently.

And, once he was finally finished with his studies, with his internship and his residency, it was his mother who was behind his attending social functions that had to do with the hospital where he worked. She had argued that it was advantageous for him to be seen, although for the life of him, he had no idea how that could possibly benefit him. He had no patience with the behind-the-scenes politics that went on at the hospital. As far as he was concerned, gladhanding and smiling would never take the place of being a good surgeon.

In his book, the former didn't matter, the latter was *all* that did.

And that was where his mother had finally gotten him. On the doctor front. She had, quite artfully, pointed out that because of new guidelines and the changing medical field, getting doctors to volunteer their services and their time was becoming more and more of a difficult endeavor.

He never saw it coming.

He'd agreed with her, thinking they were having a theoretical conversation—and then that was when his mother had hit him with specifics. She'd told him about this shelter that took in single women who had nowhere else to turn. Single women with children. She reminded him how, when his father was alive, this was the sort of thing he had done on a regular basis, rendered free medical services to those in need.

Before he was able to comment—or change the subject—his mother had hit him with her request, asking him to be the one to volunteer until another doctor could be found to fill that position at the shelter. In effect, she was asking him to *temporarily* fill in.

Or so she said.

He knew his mother, and the woman was nothing if not clever. But he was going to hold her to her word.

He planned to fill in at the shelter only on a temporary basis. A *very* temporary basis.

Mitch knew his way around surgical instruments like a pro. Managing around people, however, was a completely different story. That had always been a mystery to him.

People, one of the doctors he'd interned with had insisted, wanted good bedside manner, they wanted their hands held while being told that everything was going to turn out all right.

Well, he wasn't any good at that. He didn't hold hands or spend time talking. He healed wounds. In the long run, he felt that his patients were much better served by his choice.

This was just going to be temporary, Mitch silently promised himself, pulling up into the small parking lot before the two-story rectangular building. He'd give this place an hour, maybe ninety minutes at most, then leave. The only thing he wanted to do today was get a feel for whatever might be the physical complaints that the residents of this shelter had and then he'd be on his way home.

It was doable, he told himself. No reason to believe that it wasn't.

Getting out of his serviceable, secondhand Toyota—he'd never been one for ostentatious symbols of success—Mitch took a long look at the building he was about to enter.

It didn't look the way he imagined a homeless shelter would look. There was a fresh coat of paint on the building and an even fresher-looking sign in front of it, proclaiming it to be the Bedford Rescue Mission. A handful of daisies—white and yellow—pushed their way up and clustered around both ends of the sign. Surprisingly, he noted almost as an afterthought, there were no weeds seeking to choke out the daisies.

As he approached the front door, Mitch was vaguely aware of several pairs of eyes watching him from the windows. From the way the blinds were slanted, the watchful eyes belonged to extremely petite people—children most likely around kindergarten age, he estimated.

He sincerely hoped their mothers were around to keep them in line.

Those uncustomary, nagging second thoughts crept out again as he raised his hand to ring the doorbell.

He almost dropped it again without making contact. But then he sighed. He was here, he might as well see just how bad this was. Maybe he'd overthought it.

The moment his finger touched the doorbell, Mitch heard the chimes go off, approximating the first ten notes of a song that he found vaguely familiar, one that teased his brain, then slipped away into the mist the moment the front door was opened.

A young woman with hair the color of ripened wheat stood in the doorway, making no secret of the fact that she was sizing him up. It surprised him when he caught himself wondering what conclusion she'd reached.

"Dr. Stewart," she said by way of a greeting.

A greeting he found to be rather odd. "I know who I am, who are you?" he asked.

For such a good-looking man—and she could easily see all the little girls at the shelter giggling behind their hands over this one—he came across as entirely humorless. Too bad, Melanie thought. She'd take a sense of humor over good looks any day.

A sense of humor, in her eyes, testified to a person's humanity as well as his or her ability to identify with another person. Good looks just meant a person got lucky in the gene pool.

"Melanie McAdams," she told him, identifying herself as she stepped back and opened the door wider for him.

Mitch noticed there was a little girl hanging on to the bottom of the young woman's blouse. The girl had curly blond hair and very animated green eyes. He assumed she was the woman's daughter.

"You run this place, or live here?" he asked her bluntly.

"Neither."

Melanie's answer was short, clipped and definitely not customary for her.

She wasn't sure if she liked this man.

One thing was for certain, though. Theresa was right. He was definitely going to need someone to guide him through the ins and outs of dealing with the residents here. Especially the little residents.

She could tell by the expression on his face that he felt, justifiably or not, that he was a cut above the people who lived here. Obviously not a man who subscribed to the "There but for the grace of God go I" theory of life, Melanie thought.

It jibed with what she'd found out.

Once she'd been told the doctor's name yesterday, she'd done her homework and looked him up on the internet. The list of awards and commendations after his name went on and on, but the few photographs she could find of the doctor—and there were *very* few—showed a man who looked stiff and out of place each and every time. It seemed as if he were wishing himself somewhere else.

She supposed, in his defense, fund raisers—because those were all she'd found—could be seen as draining.

But she had a nagging feeling that the good doctor reacted that way to most people he was around. He probably felt they were all beneath him because, after all, it took a certain amount of intelligence and tenacity to study medicine and pass all those tests.

Or maybe the man was just good at memorizing things, she thought now, looking at him face-to-face. The true test of someone's ability and intelligence was putting their knowledge into action.

Hopefully, the only thing this doctor was going to be putting into action would be his stethoscope and his prescription pad when it came to writing prescriptions for antibiotics.

Once word got out that a doctor was coming to the shelter, suddenly their "sick" population had mushroomed.

Mitch raised a quizzical eyebrow, as if waiting for more information.

"I'm your guide," Melanie told him, explaining her current function.

She thought her word for it was a far more tactful label than telling the doctor that she was going to be his go-between, acting as a buffer between him and the patients he would be seeing because his reputation had preceded him—both his good reputation and the one that was not so good.

"I hope you brought your patience with you," Melanie said cheerfully. "No pun intended," she added quickly, realizing the play on words she'd just unintentionally uttered. "When word spread that you were coming, people couldn't put their names down on the sign-in sheet fast enough."

He looked at her, slightly mystified. "They know who I am?" he questioned.

Mitch didn't see how that was possible. He didn't move in the same circles as anyone who would find herself to be homeless.

He didn't move in circles at all, which was another source of distress to his mother. He preferred to spend his downtime learning new techniques, studying medical journals and observing new methodologies.

"They know that you're a doctor," she clarified. "And some of them haven't been to see one in a very long time," she said tactfully.

So saying, Melanie took hold of his elbow and gently directed him toward the left.

"That way," she said when the doctor spared her a warning look.

She couldn't help wondering if there was some sort of a penalty exacted by him for deigning to touch the man. He didn't look the least bit friendly or approachable.

But then, his competence was what was important here, not how wide his smile was. Smiles didn't cure people. Medicine, competently utilized, did—and that was all that mattered.

But a smile wouldn't have killed the man.

"We've taken the liberty of clearing the dining room for you," she informed him, still doing her best to sound cheerful.

It wasn't for his benefit, it was for April's. The little girl had literally become her shadow, hanging on to her and matching her step for step. She was observing this doctor, looking at him as if he were some sort of rarefied deity who had come to earth to make her older brother well.

"The dining hall?" he repeated as if she'd just told him that he had a complimentary pass to a brothel.

Melanie nodded, wondering what the problem was now. There was no disguising his disdain.

"It's the only room big enough to hold all the people who signed up," she explained.

Not waiting for him to say anything further, Melanie opened the dining room's double doors.

There were women and children seated at the long cafeteria-styled tables. Every seat, every space beyond that, seemed to be filled as a sea of faces all turned in his direction.

Mitch stared at the gathering, then looked at her beside him. "I was planning on staying about an hour," he told her.

"You might want to revise your plans," Melanie tactfully advised. "Some of these people have been sitting here, waiting since last night when they first heard that a doctor was coming. They didn't want to risk being at the end of the line and having you leave before they got to see you."

That was *not* the face of a man within whom compassion had just been stirred. For two cents, she'd tell him off—

More bees with honey than with vinegar, Melanie silently counseled herself.

Putting on her best supplicant expression, she decided to attempt to appeal to the man who seemed rooted to the threshold as he scanned the room.

"Is there any way you could possibly revamp your schedule and give up a little more time today?" Melanie asked him.

Like maybe three more hours?

She knew saying aloud what she was thinking wouldn't go over very well, but then, what had this doctor been thinking? He had to have known this was a homeless shelter which, by definition, meant it went literally begging for help of every kind—and that obviously included medical aid.

Medical aid was not dispensed in the same manner as drive-through fast food was.

"I know that everyone here would be very grateful if you could," Melanie said as tactfully and diplomatically as she could.

Just as she finished, another voice was added to hers.

"Please?"

The high-pitched plea came from the little girl who had been hanging on to the hem of her blouse off and on since she'd opened the front door.

April was currently aiming her 100-watt, brilliant green eyes at him.

In Melanie's estimation, Dr. Mitchell Stewart should have been a goner.

Chapter Three

To Melanie's disappointment—and growing concern—the doctor *wasn't* a goner. He did not melt beneath the pleading look in April's wide eyes.

But at least Dr. Stewart appeared to be wavering just the slightest bit, which was something.

Okay, so the man apparently didn't come with a marshmallow center beneath that tough exterior, but at least his heart wasn't made of hard rock, either, which meant that there was hope. And—except on a very personal level, where she had learned better—when it came to dealing with things at the shelter, Melanie found that she could do a lot of things and go a long way on just a smattering of hope.

Hope was like dough. It could be stretched and plumped with the right kind of preparation, not to mention the right wrist action.

She heard the doctor clear his throat. It wasn't exactly a sympathetic sound, but it wasn't entirely dismissive, either.

And then the next second she heard him say, "I'll see what I can do."

And we have lift off! Melanie thought. The man was conceding—at least a little.

She watched as Dr. Stewart looked around the dining hall, frowning at his surroundings. At first, Melanie thought he was frowning at the occupants in the room, but when he spoke, addressing his words to her, she realized that something else was bothering him.

"Don't you have anyplace more private? I'm not practicing war zone medicine," he informed her. "I don't think these women would appreciate being examined while everyone looks on, as if they were some items brought in for show-and-tell."

"Not exactly diplomatically put, but you do have a point," Melanie agreed.

When he looked at her sharply, she realized that she'd said the first part of that sentence out loud instead of just in her head. She would have to do a better job of censoring herself around this man.

Rather than apologize, she flashed him a quick smile and said, "Stay here. I'll see if I can get Polly to give up her office."

"Polly," he repeated as if he was trying to make a connection. "That would be the woman who runs this place?"

Melanie nodded. "That would be she."

"Why wasn't she out here to meet me?" he asked. The question was blunt, but she was beginning to expect that from him. She wondered if his ego had been bruised by the unintentional slight.

Melanie paused for a moment, weighing her options. She could lie to him and say they'd suddenly had an emergency on their hands that required Polly's presence, but she had a feeling that the man valued the truth above diplomacy. She also had the uneasy feeling that he could spot a lie a mile away. That cut down on her viable choices.

"Truthfully," she told him, "I think your reputation scared her."

"My reputation," he repeated slowly. "You mean the fact that I'm an above-average surgeon?"

No failure of ego to thrive here, she silently noted. "Not that reputation," she said out loud. "The other one" was all Melanie told him before she left the dining hall to track down the shelter's director.

Polly French, in her opinion, was one of the nicest people ever to walk the earth. Polly possessed a heart that was as big as she was tall and at six-one that was saying a great deal. But despite the shadow she cast, Polly was also one of the most mild-mannered people ever created. Melanie sincerely doubted if the woman even knew *how* to yell. She was certain that Polly's vocal chords weren't constructed that way.

Taking a chance that the woman was actually in her office, Melanie headed there first. She found that the door was open, but even so, Melanie stopped in front of it and knocked.

Polly, her gray hair neatly pulled back into a tight ponytail at the nape of her neck, looked up. Apprehension immediately entered the brown eyes when she saw who had knocked.

"Is something wrong, Melanie? Didn't the doctor get here yet?" she asked, rising from behind the desk, as if she was better prepared to take bad news standing up.

"He got here and there's nothing wrong," Melanie quickly assured her, then explained the reason she'd sought her out, "but I was wondering if we could borrow your office."

"Of course." Polly, ever accommodating, began to remove things from her desktop. "Isn't there enough room in the dining hall?"

"It's crammed, but so far, everyone can fit in there—but that's just the problem. The doctor thought that privacy was in order during the actual exam," she told the shelter's director. All in all, that seemed rather sensitive of him—something she did find surprising about the man.

"Oh." Caught aback, Polly rolled the thought over in her mind. "Well, that's a good sign," she commented, a small smile curving her mouth. The smile grew as she added, "He cares about their feelings."

"So it would appear," Melanie tentatively agreed, although he certainly hadn't sounded as if that was the case.

Polly picked up on her tone. "But you're reserving judgment," the woman guessed as she closed her laptop and tucked it under her arm.

"I've found it's safer that way," Melanie replied, her tone indicating that she wasn't about to elaborate on the subject in any fashion.

Polly flashed her a sympathetic smile, not unlike the one that Theresa had aimed her way the other day. She accompanied it with the same sentiment Theresa had expressed. "You know that I'm here if you need to talk, Melanie."

"I know you are," Melanie replied, definitely wanting to bring the subject to a close. She appreciated the effort, but she really wanted everyone to stop offering her shoulders and ears and various other body parts to lean on or make use of. Right now, she just wanted to get immersed in work and more work. So much work that she didn't have time to draw two breaths together, much less let herself grieve. "Can I tell the doctor he has his private room?"

"Yes, of course." She looked down at the desktop. "I'll get one of the fresh sheets out of the linen closet. That should help make this look more like an exam room," she said, thinking out loud. Then, just as Melanie began to leave the room, she asked. "Oh, did the doctor bring a nurse with him?"

"Not unless she's very, very small and fits into his pocket," Melanie replied.

"In that case, I'm going to need you to stay very close to the doctor when he's in here with a patient," Polly said.

Melanie looked at the woman uncertainly. "Come again?"

"Legally, even though he is a doctor, he can't perform an in-depth examination on any female patient without another female being present," Polly told her, looking very uncomfortable about her position. "Under normal circumstances, that would be a nurse, of course. However—"

The director definitely seemed agonized over what she was saying. Taking pity on the woman, Melanie stopped her.

"Got it. Okay," she agreed. "Don't worry, I'll stick to him like glue."

Polly headed to the linen closet while Melanie made her way back to the dining hall to inform the doctor that he had his private exam room.

The moment she walked into the hall, April lit up and gravitated to her side as if she were being propelled by a giant magnet.

Melanie barely had time to pat the little girl's head before she found herself looking into the doctor's dark blue, accusing eyes.

"I thought maybe you decided to clock out." There was no missing the touch of sarcasm in the man's voice.

Theresa wasn't kidding when she said the man was lacking in bedside manner—his would have seemed harsh when compared to Ivan the Terrible, she thought.

Out loud she told him, "Things don't happen here in a New York minute. It takes a little time to arrange things. But the director's office is ready for you to use now. So if you're ready to examine your first patient, I'll show you where it is."

He didn't answer her one way or another. Instead, he gave her an order. Orders seemed to come easily to him.

"Lead the way."

For a split second, a comeback hovered on her lips. After all, she wasn't some lackey waiting to be issued marching orders. But then she decided that the man just might get it into his head to walk out on them and while personally she didn't care, she did care about all these women and children at the shelter and they *did* need to see a doctor.

So, for now, she kept any observation to herself, much as it pained her to keep silent.

With that in mind, she turned on her heel and led the way down the hall, preceding the doctor and the woman who was to be his first patient, Jane Caldwell. Like Jimmy, Jane had a hacking cough and Melanie suspected that was possibly how Jimmy had contracted his cough in the first place.

"It's right in here," Melanie told the doctor. Pushing the door open farther, she waited for Dr. Stewart and then his patient to walk in before she followed them inside.

"There's no exam table," Mitch immediately observed, disapproval echoing in his voice.

"No." Melanie indicated the desk. "But Polly thought that you might be able to use the desktop in place of one. It's not exactly what you're used to, but it's flat and it's big," she pointed out.

He found her cheerfulness irritating. "So's your parking lot, but I'm not about to examine this woman on it."

"I'll see what I can come up with for your next visit," Melanie told him.

By the expression she saw pass over the man's face, Melanie had a feeling that the good doctor wasn't about to think that far ahead—or commit to it, either. Hopefully, once he saw how desperately a doctor's services were needed here, the man would change his mind by the end of his visit.

Melanie mentally crossed her fingers.

Still trying to convince the doctor to make do with the conditions facing him, she pointed out, "The director does have a fresh bed sheet spread over the desk. Couldn't you use that for the time being?"

"I guess I'll have to make do," he murmured under his breath, more to himself than to her. Then he said a bit louder, "All right, thanks."

His tone was dismissive.

He turned his attention to the woman who was to be his first patient here. "If you sit down on top of the desk, I can get started," he told Jane.

Mitch had already taken his stethoscope out of his medical bag and he was about to raise it in order to listen to the woman's lungs. A noise behind him made him realize that his so-called "guide" was still in the room, standing before the closed door.

Looking at her over his shoulder, he repeated what had been his parting word, "Thanks."

"You're welcome," Melanie replied, thinking that perhaps the doctor was waiting for some kind of formal acknowledgment of his thanks.

Mitch stifled an exasperated sigh .

"You can go now," he told her.

Melanie smiled patiently in response as she told him, "No, I can't."

He lowered the stethoscope. "What's that supposed to mean?"

Melanie proceeded to take his sentence apart. "Well, *no* is pretty self-explanatory. *I* refers to me and *can't* goes back to the first word, *no*," she told him glibly. "What part of those three words are you having trouble with?"

"The part that involves you." He spelled out his question for her. "Why are you still in the room?"

"Because you don't have a pocket-sized nurse with

you," she answered, following her words with another glib smile.

Did this woman have some sort of brain damage? Why was she here? Why wasn't she committed somewhere? "What?" he demanded.

"You can't examine any female without another female being present. You usually have a nurse present when you conduct your exams in the hospital, right?"

Mitch frowned. He wasn't about to argue with her because she was right, but having to concede to this woman irritated him nonetheless.

Taking a second to collect himself, Mitch barked out his first order. "Make yourself useful, then."

He expected an argument from her. Instead, the woman surprised him by asking, "And how would you like me to do that?"

The first thing that flashed through his mind was *not* something he could repeat and that surprised Mitch even more. So much so that for a second, he was speechless. He was stunned that he'd had that sort of a thought to begin with under these conditions— and that he'd had it about her, well, that stunned him even more.

"Take notes," he said, composing himself.

"Do you want me to use anything in particular in taking these notes?" she asked.

She really was exasperating. "Anything that's handy," he answered curtly, turning his attention back to the patient—or trying to.

Melanie opened the center drawer and took out a yellow legal pad and pen. Stepping back and standing a couple of feet to his left, holding the pad in one hand, she poised the pen over it and announced, "Ready when you are, Doctor."

Mitch spared her one dark glare before he began his first exam.

Like a robot on automatic pilot, Mitch saw one patient after another, spending only as much time with each one as was necessary.

Most of what he encountered over the course of the next three hours fell under the heading of routine. Some patients' complaints, however, turned out to be more complicated, and those called for lab tests before any sort of comprehensive diagnosis could be reached. The latter was necessary before any sort of medication could be dispensed.

Those Melanie marked down as needing more extensive exams.

Three hours later, feeling as if he had just been on a nonstop marathon, Mitch discovered that he had barely seen half the people who had initially lined up to be examined.

This really *was* like war-zone medicine, he couldn't help thinking.

"Do you have to go?" Melanie asked him as he sent another patient on her way. Granted she'd done an awful lot of writing in the past three hours, but she was keenly aware of the patients who were still waiting. The patients who were going to have to accept a rain check.

Mitch hadn't said anything about leaving, although he was ready to pack it in. He looked at the woman beside him in surprise. At this point, he was ready to believe she was half witch.

Maybe *all* witch.

"How did you know?" he asked her.

"Well, you said you were going to give us an hour and you've already gone two hours past that. The math isn't that challenging," she told him matter-of-factly.

Mitch frowned. They were alone in the so-called "exam room" and part of him was dealing with the very real urge of wanting to throttle her. The other part was having other thoughts that seemed to be totally unrelated to the situation—and yet weren't.

"Anyone ever tell you that you have a smart mouth on you?" he asked.

He didn't pull punches, she thought. A lot of people kept treating her with kid gloves and maybe his way was more like what she really needed—to get into a fighting mode.

"It goes with the rest of me," she answered flippantly, then got down to business. What was important here were the children and their mothers, not anything that had to do with her. "When can you come back?" she asked him.

Caught off guard, Mitch paused. "I hadn't thought about that."

In all honesty, the only thing that had been on his mind was getting through this session. As far as he was concerned, he'd fulfilled his obligation. He'd agreed to come here, as his mother had asked him to, and here he was—staying longer than he'd either intended to or wanted to. But apparently, that didn't seem to be enough.

"Maybe you should," Melanie was telling him. And then she added with a smile that appeared outwardly cheerful—but didn't fool him for a minute. "We're available anytime you are."

Mitch sighed. "I'll check my calendar."

"Why don't you do it now?" she suggested, pushing the issue. "This way, I can tell the director and your new fans out there," she nodded toward the door and the people who were beyond that, "when to expect you."

"Definitely a smart mouth," Mitch muttered as he took out his phone and checked the calendar app that was on it. His frown deepened when he found what he was looking for. "I can possibly spare a few hours Friday morning," he told her grudgingly.

She met his frown with nothing short of enthusiasm. "Friday works for us," she assured him. "I'll get the word out."

His tone was nothing if not dour when he said in response, "Why don't we wait and see how things gel?" he suggested, then qualified, "Things have a way of cropping up."

Her eyes met his and there was a defiance in them he found both irritating beyond words—and at the same time, oddly intriguing.

He supposed that maybe his mother had a point. He could stand to get out more. Then people like this annoying woman would hold no interest for him.

"Why don't you write the shelter into your schedule anyway?" she said. "Having a commitment might make you more inclined to honor it."

"Are you lecturing me?" he asked point-blank.

"I'd rather think of it as making a tactful suggestion," she replied.

She could call it whatever she wanted to, Mitch thought. But no matter what label she put on it, they both knew what she meant.

Chapter Four

Melanie looked at her watch. It was the old-fashioned, analog kind which required her brain to figure out the exact time.

Right now, the second hand seemed to be taunting her. As it moved along the dial, hitting each number one at a time, she could almost hear it rhythmically beating out: *I told you so. I told you so.*

A deep sigh escaped her.

It was Friday. The doctor should have been here by now.

She supposed, giving the man the benefit of the doubt, he could have been held up in traffic, but it would have had to have been a monumental traffic jam for Dr. Stewart to be this late. After all, it wasn't like this was Los Angeles. If anything, Bedford was considered a distant suburb of Los Angeles, located in the southern region of the considerably more laid-back Orange County area.

Granted, traffic jams did have a nasty habit of popping up in Orange County, but when they did, they had the decency of doing so between the hours of six and nine in the morning or four and seven in the evening, otherwise whimsically referred to by the term "rush hour," which was a misnomer if ever she heard one.

"Isn't he coming, Melody?" April asked her, the small voice echoing with the same concern that she herself felt. The five-year-old had decided to keep vigil with her today, unofficially appointing herself Dr. Stewart's keeper.

Melanie came away from the window. Staring out into the parking lot wasn't going to make the man appear any faster—if at all.

"I don't know, honey," she answered.

"But he said he would," April said plaintively.

It was obvious that the little girl had taken the doctor's word to be as good as a promise. But then, Melanie reminded herself, according to what she'd said, the little girl still believed in Santa Claus. Apparently the doctor's word fell into the same category as the legendary elf did.

"Yes, he did," Melanie agreed, searching for a way to let the little girl down gently. "Maybe he called Miss Polly to say he was running late."

"How can he do that?" April asked, her face scrunching up as she tried to wrap her little mind around the phrase. "If he's running, how can he be late?" she asked, confused.

"I'm afraid it's something grown-ups do all the

time, sweetie," Melanie said evasively. "Tell you what. You stay here and keep on watching for him," she instructed, turning April back toward the large window facing the parking lot. She felt having her here, standing watch, was better than having April listen in on the conversation she was going to have with the director. "I'll be right back."

"Okay!" April agreed, squaring her small shoulders as she stared out the window, as intent as any soldier standing guard. "He'll be here, I know he will," were the words that followed Melanie out of the room.

"If he's not," Melanie murmured under her breath, "I'll kill him." It would be justifiable payback for breaking April's heart.

Melanie turned the corner just as the director was walking out of her office. A near collision was barely avoided and only because Melanie's reflexes were sharp enough for her to take a quick step back before it was too late.

Her hand flying to her chest, the tall, thin woman dragged in a quick, loud breath.

"I was just coming to look for you," Polly declared breathlessly.

"Well, here I am," Melanie announced, spreading her hands wide like a performer who had executed a particularly clever dance step.

She was stalling and she knew it, Melanie thought, dropping her hands to her sides. Stalling because she didn't want to hear what she knew was coming.

Raising her head, she looked the director in the eye. "He called, didn't he?" she asked. "Dr. Stewart," she added in case her question sounded too ambiguous.

Just because she was thinking of the doctor didn't

mean that Polly was. The woman did handle all facets of the shelter, from taking in donations to finding extra beds when the shelter was already past its quota of homeless occupants. In between was everything else, including making sure there was enough food on hand as well as all the other bare necessities that running the shelter entailed.

The look in Polly's eyes was a mixture of distress and sympathy. "Just now. He said that something had come up and he couldn't make it."

Since it was already almost an hour past the time that Dr. Stewart should have been here, Melanie murmured, "Better late than never, I suppose. So when is he coming?" she asked. She wanted to be able to give April and the others a new date.

Polly shook her head. "He didn't say anything about that."

Melanie looked at her in surprise. The question came out before she could think to stop it. "You didn't ask him?"

"I didn't get a chance," Polly confessed. "I'm afraid he hung up right after saying he was sorry."

"Right," Melanie muttered under her breath. "I just bet he was."

Polly had been in charge of the shelter for a dozen years and had become accustomed to dealing with other people's disappointments as well as her own. She apparently survived by always looking at the positive side.

"We were lucky that he came when he did," she told Melanie.

But Melanie was angry. Angry at the doctor for breaking his promise to the shelter, but most of all, angry that he had in effect broken his promise to April because the little girl had taken him at his word when he'd said he was returning Friday—which was today.

"We'd be luckier if he honored his word and came back," Melanie bit off.

"A volunteer is under no legal obligation to put in any specified amount of time here," Polly pointed out. "Just because he came once doesn't mean that he has to come again."

"No, it doesn't," Melanie agreed. "But most people with a conscience would come back, especially if they said they would." Turning on her heel, she started back down the hall.

"Melanie, where are you going?" Polly called after her nervously.

"Out," Melanie answered, never breaking stride or turning around. "To cool off."

And she knew exactly how to cool off.

She slowed down only long enough to tell April that she was going to go talk to Dr. Stewart.

"Why can't you talk to him here?" April asked, following her to the front door.

There were times when April was just too inquisitive, she thought. "Because he isn't here yet and if I wait for him to get here, I might forget what I want to say to him."

"Maybe you should write it down," April piped up helpfully. "That way you won't forget."

Melanie paused at the front door and kissed the top of her unofficial shadow's head. This was the little girl she was never going to have. The kind of little girl she and Jeremy would have loved to have had as they started a family.

Tears smarted at the corners of her eyes and she blinked hard to keep them at bay. "This way is faster, trust me," she told April.

With that, she was out the door and heading to her car.

In all fairness, she knew what Polly had said was absolutely true. Mitchell Stewart had no legal obligation to show up at the shelter ever again if he didn't want to, even though he'd said he would. He'd signed no contract, was paid no stipend.

But how could a man just turn his back on people he knew were waiting for him? Didn't he have a conscience? Didn't the idea of a moral obligation mean *anything* to the man?

She gunned her car as she pulled out onto the street.

Maybe it didn't mean anything to him, but in that case, he had to find out that there *were* consequences for being so damn coldhearted. If nothing else, calling him out and telling him what she thought of him would make her feel better.

As sometimes happened, the traffic gods were on the side of the angels. Melanie made every light that was between the shelter and Bedford Memorial Hospital. Which in turn meant that she got from point A to point B in record time.

After pulling onto the hospital compound, Melanie drove the serpentine route around the main building to the small parking area in the rear reserved strictly for emergency room patients and the people who'd brought them.

Once she threw the car into Park and pulled up the emergency brake, Melanie jumped out of her vehicle

and hurried in through the double electronic doors.
They hadn't even opened up fully before she zipped
through them and into the building.

The lone receptionist at the outpatient desk glanced
up when he saw her hurrying toward him. Dressed in
blue scrubs and looking as if he desperately needed
a nap, the young man asked her, "What are you here
for?" His fingers were poised over the keyboard as
he waited for an answer to input.

"Dr. Stewart's head," she shot over her shoulder as
she hurried past him and over to the door which allowed admittance into the actual ER salon.

Ordinarily locked, it had just opened to allow a
heavyset patient to walk out, presumably on his way
home. Melanie wiggled by the man and managed to
get into the ER just before the doors shut again.

Safe for now, she buttonholed the first hospital em-
ployee she saw—an orderly—and said, "I'm looking
for Dr. Stewart." When she'd called the hospital on her
way over, she'd been told he was still on the premises,
working in the ER. "Can you tell me where he is?"

The orderly pointed to the rear of the salon. "I just
saw him going to bed 6."

"Thank you."

Melanie lost no time finding just where bed 6 was
located.

The curtain around the bed was pulled closed, no
doubt for privacy. She was angry at Stewart, not whoever was in bed 6, so she forced herself to be patient
and waited outside the curtain until the doctor was
finished.

As she stood there, listening, she found that Dr.
Stewart was no more talkative with the hospital pa-

tients than he was with the women and children he'd examined at the shelter.

It occurred to her that if he was like this all the time, Dr. Stewart had to be one very lonely, unhappy man. Obviously he was living proof that no matter how bad someone felt they had it, there was always someone who had it worse.

In her opinion, Dr. Mitch Stewart was that some-one.

Mitch had been at this all morning. Rod Wilson, who had the ER shift right after his, had called in sick. Most likely, Wilson was hung over. The man tended to like to party. But that didn't change the fact that he wasn't coming in and that left the hospital temporarily short one ER doctor. Which was why he'd agreed to take Wilson's place after his own shift was over.

As far as he was concerned, this unexpected event was actually an omen. He wasn't meant to go back to the shelter, this just gave him the excuse he needed.

He'd felt out of his element there anyway, more so than usual. Here at least he was familiar with his surroundings and had professional people at his disposal in case he needed help with one of the patients.

That wasn't the case at the shelter and even though he knew his strengths and abilities, he didn't care for having to wing it on his own. Too many things could go wrong.

Finished—he'd closed up a small laceration on the patient's forearm caused by a wayward shard from a broken wine glass—Mitch told the patient a nurse would be by with written instructions for him regarding the proper care of his sutures.

With that, he pulled back the curtain and walked out.

Or tried to.

What he wound up doing was walking right into the annoying woman from the homeless shelter.

His eyes narrowed as recognition instantly set in. "You."

He said the single word as if it were an accusation.

"Me," she responded glibly.

Since he'd started walking, she fell into place beside him. She wasn't about to let him get away, at least not until she gave him a piece of her mind—or a chance to redeem himself, whichever he chose first.

Mitch scowled at her as he pulled off the disposable gloves from his hands. "You realize that this is bordering on stalking, don't you?"

Her eyes narrowed into slits. "You're not at the shelter."

"Mind like a steel trap," he marveled sarcastically. He paused to drop his gloves into a covered garbage container. "Tell me, what gave you your first clue?"

There were things she wanted to say to him, retorts aimed straight at his black heart, but she had to make sure first that there wasn't the slimmest possibility that he could be convinced to come back with her.

She gave him one last chance. "There's a room full of people waiting for you."

Mitch frowned. "Didn't your director give you the message? I called," he told her.

"After the fact," she pointed out since he had called almost an hour after he should have been at the shelter.

"Better than not at all," Mitch said sharply, wondering why he was even bothering to have this discussion with this annoying woman. He didn't owe her any explanations.

"Better if you came back with me," she countered, going toe-to-toe with him.

Her display of gall completely astounded him.

"Better than what?" he asked. And then his eyes widened. "Are you by any chance actually threatening me?"

She would have loved to, but she was neither bigger than Dr. Stewart was nor did she have anything on the doctor to use as leverage, so she resorted to the only tactic she could.

"I'm appealing to you," she retorted.

"Not really," Mitch shot back.

The moment the words were out of his mouth— and he was glad he'd had the presence of mind to say them—he realized that they actually weren't true. Because, strangely enough, she *did* appeal to him. What made it worse was that he hadn't a clue as to why.

If he'd had a type, which he'd long since not had, it wouldn't have been a mouthy little blonde who didn't know when to stop talking. He liked tall, sleek brunettes with tanned complexions, dark, smoldering eyes and long legs that didn't quit. Women who kept their own counsel rather than making him want to wrap his hands around their throats to stop the endless flow of words coming out of their mouths.

So why the contradiction in his head?

He told himself the double shift had made him more tired than usual. He just wasn't being his usual, reasonable self.

"They need you," Melanie insisted as she continued to follow him down a corridor.

"They need a doctor," he corrected.

His intent was to show her it wasn't personal, that anyone would do and that it didn't have to be him. Furthermore, *wasn't* going to be him because at this point he just wanted to take a shower and go home.

He kept walking. So did she.

"Last I checked, that was you."

He stopped just short of his destination—the locker room. At the last moment, she held herself in check to keep from colliding with him.

"Look, how about if I get you someone else?" he suggested.

"I've always been a great believer in the bird in the hand school of thought," Melanie told him.

This actually might have been amusing if she weren't so damn annoying. "I'm neither a bird, nor am I in your hand," he told her tersely.

"No, but you're here, you're a doctor, and you've already been to the shelter." As if to drive her point home, she said, "The kids saw you."

"They've probably seen a SpongeBob SquarePants movie, too," he said, exasperated. "Would you want him to be their doctor?"

She looked at him, wondering if maybe she was pushing too hard. The next moment, she decided that he was just trying to confuse her and get her to back off.

Taking a breath, she tried another approach. Softening her tone, she said, "Please? They're at the shelter, waiting and right now, they're waiting for you." And then she gave it to him with both barrels. "Somewhere along the line, when you first started studying to be a doctor, didn't you want someone to be waiting for you to come and save the day?"

He laughed shortly at the image she was attempting to promote. "You mean like a superhero?"

"No," she corrected, "like a super-doctor."

Just then, a man in a security uniform approached them. Specifically, Melanie noted, the guard was approaching *her*.

"Is there a problem here?" the security guard asked, looking from her to the doctor. His hand was resting rather dramatically on the hilt of his holstered weapon as he waited for an answer.

All he had to do, Mitch thought, was say yes and this annoying woman would be out of his hair once and for all. But he had to admit—grudgingly so— that there was a germ of truth in what she'd just said. Once, when he was still very young and very idealistic, he'd had great hopes for the profession he was aspiring to. His head—and his heart—had been filled with thoughts of what he could accomplish.

In those days, he'd been inspired by what his father had accomplished before him. Though he'd never said as much, back then, his father had been his idol and he'd wanted to be just like him.

All it had taken was losing a couple of patients to show him how wrong—and foolhardy—he had been. At the end of the day, all he could hope for was the same amount of wins as losses.

"No," he finally said to the guard, "there's nothing wrong. She was just reminding me of an appointment I'd forgotten about."

The guard looked somewhat dubious. "If you're sure everything's all right…"

"I'm sure," Mitch told him.

"Okay, then," the guard murmured. "Have a nice day.

And with that, he withdrew.

Melanie gazed at the man she had come to drag back to the shelter. "Thank you."

"Yeah," he muttered. "I'll probably live to regret that." He started to push open the door behind him. When he saw that his self-appointed conscience was about to come in with him, he said, "Unless you plan to suddenly join the staff, you can't come in here."

Was he going to evade her after all? "Why not?" she asked.

"Because it's the locker room."

"Oh." She suddenly realized he was right. "Sorry."

Was she blushing? It didn't seem possible. These days, everything was so blatant, so out in the open, he doubted if anyone blushed over anything. It was probably just the poor lighting.

Mitch jerked a thumb behind him toward the locker room. "I'm just going to go take a shower and change out of these scrubs."

"Fine," she responded, then, in case there was any doubt, she added, "I'll be out here, waiting."

Mitch made no verbal comment, he merely grunted in response to her affirmation. It never occurred to him to think that she wouldn't be.

Chapter Five

Tucking away the supplies he'd brought with him into his medical bag, Mitch didn't even hear the knock at first. When the sound continued, more insistently this time, he glanced up, bracing himself.

Now what?

He'd already spent forty-five minutes more than he'd anticipated at the shelter and he really didn't want to get roped into anything else that would prevent him from leaving—always a viable possibility whenever that woman, Melanie, was involved. Over the course of the past month, that lesson had been driven home more than once. Even a slow learner would have picked up on that by now and he was far from that.

Anticipation mixed with dread filtered through him when he saw Melanie walking into the alcove that she'd persuaded the director to turn into a permanent exam room—or as permanent as anything could be here in the homeless shelter. Slightly larger than a linen closet, it had room for the necessary examination table and just enough room for him to move around in.

Any sort of lengthy conversation resulting from an exam, however, still took place in the director's office. Polly willingly surrendered her office to him whenever he came to the shelter.

Lately, that was two, sometimes three times a week and never for as short a duration as he initially anticipated.

As he watched Melanie approach him, his attention was drawn to what she was carrying. His eyes narrowed and he nodded at what she'd brought into the room. "What's this?"

"It's a cake," she told him. Then, still leaving it on the tray she'd used to bring it in, she placed the whole thing on the exam table right in front of him. "Well, actually," she amended, "it's a large cupcake."

He had to learn to be more specific when he asked questions, Mitch told himself—at least when it came to things that had to do with Melanie.

"I *know* what it is. I want to know what it's doing on a plate in front of me with a candle in it. A *lit* candle," he underscored.

"Waiting for you to blow out the flame," she told him with a smile that he was finding increasingly difficult to ignore each time he saw it. The reason for *that* he refused to explore.

He made no move to do as she'd just instructed, not until he knew what he was getting himself into. When it came to Melanie, the more information he had before he got further involved, the better. And even then, he wasn't always fully prepared. The woman was just *not* predictable.

"Any particular reason you have this sudden need to set a cupcake on fire?" he asked.

Her smile was patient—and he found it so much more annoying because of that.

"I'm not setting it on fire," Melanie told him. "It's to celebrate—"

"—your one month annie-versay," April piped up excitedly, coming out from behind Melanie.

The next moment she giggled into her hands as if she'd just played some sort of a fine joke on the solemn-faced doctor—whom she obviously really liked despite the rather somber expression he usually wore.

Then, in case the significance of what she'd just said had escaped him, April proudly announced, "You've been coming here a whole month!" She made it sound like a feat equal to coming in first in the Kentucky Derby. "Make a wish and blow it out!" she urged excitedly.

He knew there was no way he was getting out of here until he complied with this nonsense, so he put his medical bag down on the floor. Leaning over the exam table, Mitch slanted a glance toward the woman who'd brought in the cupcake—and him, he thought grudgingly—in the first place. Then, none-too-happily, he blew out the candle.

"A month, huh?" he repeated as if the fact was just now registering in his brain. "Funny," he said, looking directly at Melanie, "it seems longer."

"Funny, I was just going to say that it doesn't really feel that long at all," Melanie deliberately countered.

"But then," she allowed, "I wasn't the one who was dragged here, kicking and screaming."

"Who was kicking and screaming?" April wanted to know, a puzzled expression on her small oval face as her eyes grew large.

Melanie ruffled her hair affectionately. "It's just an expression, honey."

April appeared to be only half listening. Her attention, as well as her eyes, was fixed on the large cupcake. After a moment, she shifted both over toward Mitch.

"Aren't you going to eat that?" she asked. "I helped Melody make it."

He didn't want to insult the little girl, but he didn't want to hang around, either. It seemed that the longer he stayed—the longer he stayed.

"Tell you what," Mitch suggested, thinking he had come up with the perfect solution. "Why don't you eat it for me? You like cupcakes, right?"

"Very much," April told him, solemnly nodding her head. And then she pinned him with her large, soulful eyes. "Don't you?"

"Yes, yes I do," he told her, gathering up his medical bag again, his body poised for flight. He deliberately avoided looking in Melanie's direction. "But I'm kind of in a hurry."

April's eyes just grew more soulful. "You're always in a hurry. Don't you wanna stop some time?" she asked.

The logic of children confounded him. He was in over his head.

Mitch finally looked toward the woman who had roped him into doing all this, volunteering his services in a place he must have passed a hundred times in his travels through the city without having noticed even once. She owed him.

"Help me out here," he requested.

Melanie spread her hands wide. "Sorry, I'm kind of curious to hear your answer to that one," she replied.

As always, she ended her statement with a smile, a smile that was beginning to burrow a hole in his gut, working its way through the layers he had applied around himself over the years. Layers that were meant to insulate him from everything and anything so that he could concentrate strictly on doing what he had been educated and trained to do—being an excellent surgeon. To him that meant dedication—and isolation.

Right now, that didn't seem to be enough.

Feeling cornered and outmaneuvered by a five-year-old and her older sidekick, Mitch stifled his exasperation and just sighed in temporary surrender.

"Okay, I'll have some of the cupcake—as long as you have the rest," he said to April. "Deal?"

The sunny little face that came up to his belt buckle lit up even more. "Deal!" April cried.

"I just happen to have a knife, a couple of paper plates and a couple of forks right here," Melanie told her reluctant celebrant, producing said items almost out of thin air.

"Of course you do," Mitch murmured under his breath. He saw April looking at him as if she was trying to understand something. Deciding to get in front of whatever was brewing, he asked, "What?"

"You do that a lot," April told him with a small, disapproving frown.

"Do what?" he asked. He wasn't aware of doing anything out of the ordinary.

"Talk little, like you're whispering to somebody," April answered.

Melanie thought that was a very apt description of the way the doctor mumbled under his breath whenever he disapproved of something. She'd caught him at it a number of times.

"Out of the mouths of babes," Melanie said with a laugh. "Literally."

April surprised her by taking exception to that. "I'm not a baby," she protested.

"You certainly are not," Melanie agreed with feeling, doing her best to keep a straight face.

Cutting the cupcake in half, she split it between the sunny little girl and the dour-faced doctor.

Mitch looked at the two plates, then at her. "Why aren't you having any?" he asked.

She pointed out the obvious. "There's not all that much to go around."

Mitch did the same—or so he believed. "You could have made a bigger cake. Can't be that much more work involved."

"Then I would have had to invite other people here to share it and I don't think you're socialized enough for that," she said bluntly. "At least, I didn't think you'd appreciate me making a fuss over you in front of other people."

The woman was right, he wouldn't have liked that, although he had to admit he was surprised that she actually realized that.

"I didn't know you were that insightful," he commented.

"Lots of things about me you don't know," Melanie responded. She caught a movement out of the corner of her eyes on the exam table. "April, don't you like the cupcake?" she asked.

The little girl had pushed away her plate and moved it so that it was in front of Melanie. There was still a quarter of the cupcake left on it.

The blond head bobbed up and down with feeling. "Very much."

That didn't make any sense to her. "Then why didn't you finish it?"

The small face was utterly guileless as she said, "'Cause I wanted to share it with you."

Melanie had no idea why the little girl's answer caused tears to form in the corners of her eyes, but it took her a second before she could regain control.

Clearing her throat, she told April, "That's very sweet, honey. Tell you what, why don't you take this to Jimmy? I'm sure he'd like to have some, too."

The suggestion met with total approval. "Okay." Scooping up the plate with both hands, April flashed a huge smile at both of them, said, "Happy Annie-versary!" again and took off.

Mitch watched the little girl hurry down the hall with her prize. He also sounded wistful as he commented, "If everyone was like her, this would be a much better world."

Melanie stifled a sigh. "No argument," she responded.

Finished with his share of the cupcake, Mitch pushed the plate aside and laughed shortly. "Well, that's a first."

"And the moment's gone," Melanie declared. Taking the empty plate and putting it on top of the one that had initially held the cupcake along with its candle, she told Mitch, "Well, I won't keep you—"

"Also a first," he couldn't help commenting. "Must be some kind of a record."

Melanie paused to give him a deep, penetrating look, one that silently said she saw right through him. "You make it sound like you don't want to be here."

Didn't exactly take a rocket scientist to figure that one out, Mitch thought. Out loud, he pointed out, "Not exactly my first choice for extracurricular work," he told her flippantly.

Her eyes met his. "Bluster all you want, Doctor Mitch, but we both know that if you didn't want to be here, you *wouldn't* be here. Maybe you've noticed that you're not exactly handcuffed to a radiator."

"Bluster?" he echoed, taking offense at the minor insult rather than the larger picture she'd just painted. "I don't bluster."

To which she merely smiled. "Remind me to bring a tape recorder with me and run it the next time you're here. I think you just might need to actually listen to yourself speak—or grunt as the case may be. It just might change your mind about that denial."

The woman was beginning to sound as if she made her living as a lawyer. And then it occurred to him that he *didn't* know all that much about her—not that he had wanted to in the first place. But now that he was stuck coming back here, he figured he might as well know as much about his enemy as possible. One never knew when information like that might come in handy. Considering who he was up against, he might just need it for counter-blackmail somewhere down the line.

"What is it that you do when you're not bending steel in your bare hands and championing the underdog?" he asked.

Melanie froze for a moment and then tried to behave as if nothing had happened. But he had detected the slight change and wondered about it.

"What do you mean?"

He really doubted that she needed it spelled out for her, but he obliged, wondering at the same time why she was stalling. "Well, everyone here, except for the director, is volunteering their time away from their regular job. I was just wondering what your regular job was?"

"Diva at the Metropolitan Opera House," she told him brightly.

"I thought as much." And then Mitch grew serious. "No, really, what are you?"

"Cornered right now," she told him crisply. Plates and utensils in hand, she headed to the door. "And I've got work to do, so happy one month anniversary and if you'll excuse me—"

With that, she suddenly turned away and left him standing in the room, staring after her. Wondering more questions about the woman than he was really comfortable about wondering.

Mitch wasn't the type to ask questions that weren't directly related to a patient's condition. He didn't bother getting involved in a patient's private life, didn't entangle himself in the deeper layers that could be unearthed once a few probing questions were actually asked.

So no one was more surprised than he was when he found himself seeking out the shelter's director rather than just going out to his car in the parking lot and taking off.

It wasn't as if time hung heavily on his hands. He had more than enough to do to fill up every spare moment of the day *and* night.

But there he was, knocking at the director's door, silently calling himself an idiot and just maybe certifiably crazy.

"Yes?" the woman's voice inquired from within the office.

All thoughts of making a quick getaway and pretending this slip had never happened instantly faded when the door opened and the director looked at him with a welcoming, inquisitive smile.

He might as well see this through, Mitch thought. "You have a minute?" he asked the woman.

"For you, Doctor, always," Polly responded cheerfully. She gestured for him to come in and take a seat before her desk. Crossing back to her side, she sat down herself. "Is something wrong?" she asked with concern once he was seated.

"No, nothing's wrong," he answered.

Yeah, something's wrong. Melanie's rubbing off on me, making me ask questions I shouldn't be asking, shouldn't even want to know the answers to. Just being around her is messing with my head and I don't like it.

Mitch forced a smile he didn't feel to his lips. "I just had question. But if you don't have any time—"

he began, rising again. All he wanted was to make a quick retreat and pretend this never happened— because it shouldn't have.

"I have time," she assured him.

So much for a quick retreat.

"Please, sit. Stay," Polly encouraged, waiting for him to do both. Folding her hands before her on her desk, the thin woman leaned forward slightly, giving him every indication that he had her complete and un-divided attention. "Now, please, tell me. What's your question, Doctor?"

He felt like an idiot. A self-conscious, awkward idiot.

What did he care what Melanie did for a living? When he got right down to it, it was really none of his business *what* Melanie did for a living or even *if* she did anything for a living except come here, oc-cupy herself with the women and children who were staying here—and of course, also appointing herself as his unofficial conscience, pricking at it whenever, in her judgment, he wasn't keeping on the true path as she saw it.

Her real calling, now that he thought about it, was to be a royal pain in his posterior—and she did that with aplomb.

The silence stretched out. Rather than take it as an omen and say that perhaps they could talk another time, the director seemed to take her cue from it and head in an entirely different direction with it.

"Please, Dr. Stewart, whatever you say here will stay here, I assure you." Polly lowered her voice, as if that would get her point across more effectively. "You've been a complete godsend to these women and children and anything I can do or say, even in the slightest way, to show our utmost appreciation, well, all I can tell you is that you'd be doing me a favor rather than putting me out."

The director wasn't going to let up, he could tell. It seemed to be a common malady among the female population in this facility.

With an inward sigh, Mitch asked his question. "I was just wondering if Ms. McAdams has a job outside of the volunteer work she does here."

"She came to us as an elementary school teacher," Polly said proudly. Her smile was warm as she added, "That's why she's so good with the children here. It's her background."

Volunteering here had taught him to listen more closely than he was normally accustomed to. It made him catch things he would have previously ignored or, more to the point, overlooked.

"You said she 'came to you' as a teacher. Isn't she one now?"

"Melanie took a leave of absence after…" Polly's voice trailed off. She gave no indication that she was eager to pick up the thread she'd intentionally dropped.

Which just served to arouse his curiosity, something he would have sworn just a month ago that he'd learned to eradicate from his life. Obviously he hadn't erased it; he'd merely painted over it and it was apparently alive and well, just waiting to wake up.

Something else he could hold against Melanie.

"After?" Mitch asked. "After what?"

Polly sighed. "Well, I suppose it's really not a secret. Melanie will probably tell you herself once she feels ready to address the subject. She only told me because I needed something for the record," Polly explained.

"Go on," he urged, trying to sound patient—which he wasn't.

Why did women have this annoying habit of drawing things out like it was dough and pausing at the most inappropriate times?

"Melanie's fiancé, Jeremy, was killed while in the service overseas. It happened just four days before he was scheduled to fly back to the States for their wedding. It hit her very hard," she confided. "Melanie didn't feel that she had the right frame of mind to teach impressionable young children. Her contact with them here at the shelter is informal and that's better for her right now. And, of course, the children adore her and selfishly, I don't know what I would do without her." Polly paused, unofficially closing the subject. "Does that answer your question for you?"

"Yes," Mitch told her, rising to his feet. "It does. Thank you for your time."

"And we thank you for yours," Polly called after his departing back.

But, his mind elsewhere, Mitch was already out of earshot.

Chapter Six

"So? Tell me," Charlotte enthusiastically urged her son.

It had been over a month since she'd talked him into volunteering at the homeless shelter that Maizie had told her about. She hadn't heard from Mitch in all that time. After waiting as patiently as she could, she had decided to take matters into her own hands. Step one was inviting him out to lunch at the restaurant that was near Bedford Memorial.

Step two was getting him to actually talk. Step two was harder than step one.

When Mitch made no response to her question, she tried again. Getting information out of her son took skill and patience.

Lots of patience.

"How is it?" Charlotte pressed, doing her best not to sound impatient.

As if hearing her for the first time, Mitch raised his eyes from the sirloin steak he was enjoying and looked at his mother quizzically. He wasn't sure what she was asking.

There was no question that he loved his mother. Charlotte Stewart was and had always been a kind, decent woman who could have easily served as a prototype model for the perfect mother in all those old-fashioned sitcoms that used to litter the airwaves when he was a kid.

That being said, there were times when he just couldn't seem to understand what wavelength his mother was on.

Or maybe he was the one who was on the wrong wavelength. In either case, there were many times that he and his mother couldn't seem to make a proper connection and he felt bad about that. Bad because he knew that she meant well and she truly wanted nothing more for him than his happiness.

The problem was, he wasn't sure just what that was, or these days even what "happiness" meant. At least, not where he was concerned.

Hard to achieve something if you didn't know what it was even if you tripped over it, Mitch thought philosophically.

"It?" he repeated. No enlightenment came with the repetition. Mitch had no idea what she was referring to, but assumed it had to be something in his immediate surroundings. "You mean the steak?" he asked, indicating what he'd ordered for lunch. He hadn't realized how hungry he was until he'd taken his first bite. There was hardly anything left of the meal.

But she hadn't appeared out of the blue and whisked

him off to lunch just to find out how he liked the steak in this restaurant.

Had she?

Mitch continued to look at his mother, waiting for further enlightenment.

"No, dear, I'm talking about your volunteer work at the homeless shelter," she said patiently, then repeated, "How is it?"

She was genuinely curious about his reaction to what he both did and observed at the shelter. Curious, too, on an entirely different level if Mitch had had any sort of a reaction to the young woman Maizie had told her about, thanks to her friend Theresa. So curious that for the past two nights, she'd hardly slept, wondering how things were—or weren't—coming along.

Many years ago, when Mitch had been about five or six years old, she had made herself a vow that she wasn't going to be like all the other mothers. She wasn't going to be the kind of mother whose offspring cringed at the sound of her voice or the sight of her name on his caller ID. She wanted to be a welcomed participant in her son's life, not one he sought to avoid.

That meant, for the most part, not taking on a supervisory position when it came to what went on in Mitch's private life.

But as the years went by, it became clearer and clearer to her that as far as his life went, there really wasn't anything for her to participate *in*. Mitch was all about his work.

And when he wasn't working, he was reading up on the latest studies that were being made in his field.

She realized that she was very lucky to have a son who was intelligent, who had a profession he was absorbed in. She had friends who lamented that their son or daughter partied too much, or spent money as if they had their own printing press stored away in their spare bedroom. Others had adult offspring who acted as if they were still children, focused only on themselves and indiscriminately gratifying all their own whims and extravagances.

She knew she had a hundred reasons to be grateful that Mitchell was the way he was, but human nature being what *it* was, she couldn't help wanting something more—for him rather than for herself—because someday, she would be gone and she wanted him to have someone in his life who meant something to him. Someone he could laugh with and talk with, or simply just *be* with, sharing a room and a comfortable silence with.

Left to his own devices, she knew he'd never reach that goal she had for him. Which was why she'd decided to secretly take matters into her own hands. And now she needed to know how that was going. Needed to know if she had cause for hope—or cause for remorse.

Mitch shrugged carelessly. "Frustrating," he finally admitted, summing up his feelings in a single word. He didn't believe in using three words when one would more than adequately do.

"Why?"

Frustrating wouldn't have been the first word she would have expected to hear as a reaction from Mitch. She looked at him. Getting information out of him was like pulling teeth. Impacted teeth. "What's frustrating about it?"

It seemed almost funny to him that the first thing

he thought of in response to his mother's question was the name of the woman who was supposed to act as his assistant at the shelter—or whatever it was that Melanie saw herself as being.

He refrained from mentioning her because he knew his mother wasn't asking about a person, she was asking about how he felt about the conditions he found there. Even as a doctor's son, he hadn't exactly grown up in the lap of luxury. But even despite his father's untimely and all-too-early death, he had never actually felt the pinch of deprivation. What he saw at the shelter—and what he found himself listening to because sometimes his patients talked even when he hadn't asked them anything—had left a dark, lasting impression on him.

"Frustrating because there are free clinics located throughout the state and yet a lot of these kids at the shelter have never even had the most common immunizations. This isn't a developing nation." He realized he sounded as if he was lecturing and he toned down his voice. "Their mothers should know better."

Charlotte smiled to herself. Maybe Mitch hadn't connected with that woman—yet—but he had at least found something to be passionate about. She could see it in his eyes. That was the first, important step, she couldn't help thinking. At this singular moment in time, he reminded her very much of her late husband. Matthew would have been pleased.

With luck, the rest would follow.

"Sometimes people just fall through the cracks, dear. That's why I urged you to volunteer at the shelter in the first place," she told her son. "If you wind up helping at least one person there for no other reward than just because it's the decent thing to do, then you've done a very good thing and I will have done my part in raising you right."

Finished eating, he retired his knife and fork and studied his mother quietly. Had he missed something? "You make it sound like you're signing off from the job," he observed.

Charlotte was quick to flash her son a reassuring smile. "Not by a long shot, but none of us know how long we have. Your father thought he was going to live forever, and it didn't quite work out that way," she noted sadly. "I wanted you to experience the feeling of making a real difference in someone's life—sooner rather than later," she emphasized. "These women and children at the shelter, they desperately need someone like you making them feel as if they matter."

"Where's this coming from, Mom?"

"From the heart," she answered without a moment's hesitation. "I just wanted to make sure you had one—a heart," she said in case she'd lost him. "You've been too removed, too distant of late."

"I've been busy," he said pointedly.

Just because Bedford had one of the country's lowest crime rates for a city of its size did not mean that all he ever got to see were cuts and bruises. Some of the things that came into the ER definitely challenged him as a doctor as well as a surgeon.

"I know," Charlotte said soothingly. "But I didn't want you to lose the common touch."

"I never had the common touch, Mother," Mitch reminded her. He made sure of that because something like that, the common touch, left him open to grieving over the lives that were lost on his operating table, had him grieving over the lives he couldn't ultimately save.

He was a better doctor by keeping himself in check and removed.

But his mother obviously didn't see it that way. "All right, then it's high time that you developed it."

Charlotte could see that her son didn't look overly happy about the direction the conversation had taken and she didn't want to irritate him to the point that he was rethinking his volunteer work altogether.

She glanced at the watch he'd given her three Christmases ago. The one she never took off except when she showered—it was her small way of keeping him close to her.

"Well," she announced briskly, putting down her own fork beside her empty salad bowl, "I seem to have monopolized you for too long again. Looks like you need to get back to work, dear," she said, tapping the face of her wristwatch.

Moving his chair back, Mitch dug into his pocket for his wallet.

Charlotte placed her hand on his arm, stopping him before he had a chance to pull the wallet out.

"No, this is my treat, dear," she insisted. "I dragged you out of the hospital, the least I can do is pay for the privilege of seeing my only son for lunch."

Mitch sighed. "You don't have to pay for it and it's not a 'privilege,' Mom," he told her, trying to keep his voice down.

He didn't want to draw any undue attention, but his

mother could irritate him in a relatively short amount of time despite all of her good intentions.

Rather than back off, Charlotte affectionately laughed at her son and firmly held her ground. "Don't argue with me, dear. I gave you life. Certain rights go along with that little parlor trick."

She gathered her things together, intending on walking as far as the cashier with him. To make sure he wouldn't attempt to make off with the bill and pay it, she held it in her hand.

"This was fun," she told Mitch. "Maybe we can do this again soon."

He was open to that. "Sure." Mitch paused to kiss the top of his mother's head. "Just without the interrogation this time."

Charlotte paused, stopping just short of the cashier's desk. "What interrogation?" she asked him innocently.

Mitch almost laughed out loud. "You are definitely going to have to work on your delivery, Mom. That was *not* at all convincing."

She was in too deep to back down now, Charlotte thought. Besides, if she made any admissions, he would be within his rights to ask her more questions. She couldn't answer any of those without throwing the plan in jeopardy.

So she said the only thing she could. She embraced ignorance. "I have no idea what you mean."

Mitch merely grinned. If he'd had any doubts before, they were all gone now. His mother was engaged in something, something he would undoubtedly find annoying and which would, more than likely, add a severely complicating factor to his life. "Uh-huh."

* * *

As he hurried back to the hospital and the remainder of his shift, it occurred to Mitch that there was a lot about his mother and the way she operated that unfortunately reminded him of the woman volunteering on a permanent basis at the shelter. The annoying one with the light blue eyes and the smart mouth that never seemed to stop moving.

Not that his mother and Melanie looked anything like one another, but there was something about his mother's attitude that immediately made him think of Melanie—except that his mother was a lot kinder.

It wasn't that Melanie wasn't kind, he amended silently. Melanie was just somehow *sharper.* He guessed that was the best word to describe her attitude. Not that her mind was sharp but her tongue certainly was.

Parking his vehicle, he got out and then, as his last thoughts played back in his head, he stopped short just before he walked in through the hospital's rear double doors.

What the hell was he doing, thinking about that woman's attitude?

Or thinking about that woman, period?

Judging by the amount of vehicles he'd just passed in the rear parking lot, he had a full four hours ahead of him. That meant that there would be no downtime for him to think about the shelter or the woman who immediately popped up in his head the second his thoughts turned in that direction.

The time to think about the shelter, Mitch told himself, continuing to walk into the hospital, was when he was actually *at* the shelter.

The time to think about Melanie was *never.*

* * *

"Why do you do it?"

The question was directed to Melanie two days and five hours later.

He'd arrived at the shelter five hours ago, intending on staying roughly two hours this time around. He was immediately caught up with one patient after another. It seemed like being engulfed in an endless rushing stream. He quickly found out the reason why.

There were several new residents at the shelter. Among them were two little boys who, along with their mother, had been diagnosed with the most pronounced case of lice Mitch could ever remember not only seeing, but reading about.

Consequently, everyone had to be treated for lice as a preventative measure, even the ones who had no signs of it and loudly protested being subjected to both the exam and the harsh soap necessary to ensure that they would not be unwilling participants in the infestation.

The past five hours had been a nonstop flurry of activity and he'd reached a point where he felt it was never going to let up.

But it did.

And when it finally began to let up, Melanie momentarily vanished from his side. When he didn't see her, Mitch just assumed that she'd gone to take a well deserved break, possibly even a quick nap, something he caught himself longing for.

So he was surprised when she'd returned a few minutes later with a tall travel mug filled with coffee. Melanie pressed the mug into his hands when he had just looked at her quizzically.

After taking a long, life-affirming mouthful and swallowing it, he began to feel a little more human. A second swallow had him looking very thoughtfully at Melanie.

Since the onslaught of children had let up, he'd allowed himself to sit down on the stripped exam table. She had proceeded to join him, sitting down, producing her own smaller mug of light coffee and silently taking a drink.

The question he'd addressed to her came after he felt, thanks to her, more like himself.

Thoughts of his conversation over lunch with his mother had prompted him to ask Melanie the simple question which, he knew, didn't really have a simple answer.

Holding her mug in both hands, she looked at him a little uncertainly. "Excuse me?"

"Why do you do it?" he repeated. "Why do you come here day after day, ministering to these people the way you do?"

He knew it had to be draining—and she certainly wasn't getting paid for this. He wanted to understand what motivated her to keep coming back.

"I guess the simple answer is that someone has to," she replied in an offhand manner.

He wasn't sure if he was buying that. "What's the less simple answer?" Mitch asked. "Do you see this as some kind of penance?"

Her eyebrows drew together in a mystified line. "Penance?" she echoed, completely at a loss as to what he was really asking.

"Yes." The notion stuck in his head and the more he thought about it, the more fitting it seemed to him.

"You know, 'I feel guilty because my life is so much better than theirs is so I need to do something to assuage that guilt I'm feeling.'"

Melanie looked at him as if he'd lost his mind. She wasn't altogether sure that he hadn't.

"I don't feel guilt," she said indignantly. "I feel compassion." Taking a breath, she forced herself to calm down a bit. "Yes, I can pay my rent and I don't worry where my next meal is coming from—at least, not at this point," she interjected, thinking of her ever-shrinking bank account. Eventually, she would have to get back into the work force to resuscitate her earning power. "But I just want to help other people feel that there's always hope, that they shouldn't give up, not on life, not on themselves."

She paused, looking at him. "Are you here because you feel some sort of guilt or need for atonement?" she asked, turning the tables on him. After all, why else would he have phrased his question like that if he wasn't experiencing the same thing himself?

He should have realized that she would try to use what he asked to try to analyze him. "I'm here because it makes my mother happy."

She waved her hand at what he'd just said. He was playing a game of smoke and mirrors, which was fine, except that he wanted true confessions from her while he wanted to maintain his aura of mystery.

"That's just an excuse. You definitely don't strike me as a mama's boy."

"Okay," he said gamely, his curiosity aroused. "You seem like such an expert. Why *am* I here?"

"For the same reason I am," she told him, referring to what she'd already told him was her reason

for being here. "The only reason you won't admit it
is because you seem to think that saying so damages
the image you have of yourself." She shrugged, pausing for more coffee before adding, "Maybe it even
makes you seem too human and for some reason, you
want to see yourself—and have the world see you—as
some kind of cold, distant robot." Her eyes met his.
"And you're not."

"What makes you so sure?"

She sat there beside him, drinking her coffee and
lightly swinging her legs to and fro like a woman
without a care in the world instead of one whom life
had beaten down—or tried to.

Humor curved the corners of her mouth as she told
him, "I can just tell."

Mitch laughed shortly, shaking his head. "If you
say so."

It was meant to be dismissive. He was in no way
prepared for the ambush that happened next.

Nor was he prepared for the reaction that occurred
in its wake.

Chapter Seven

One moment Mitch was amused by this steamroller's naive presumption that she felt she knew him better than he knew himself, the next he had turned his head in her direction at the same time that she had turned her face up to his.

For a fleeting moment, it made him think of a flower turning toward its source of light.

However he saw it or tried to describe it to himself, the bottom line was that somehow, their faces wound up being less than an inch away from each other.

Close enough for him to breathe in the breath that Melanie had just exhaled.

Close enough for him to share that same breath with her.

Close enough for their lips to almost touch.

And then they did touch.

To Mitch's astonishment, there was no more space. There was just them.

If the fate of the world depended on his memory of how it had happened—whether he was the one to breach that infinitesimal space or if she was—he wouldn't have been able to say.

All he knew was suddenly, there they were, with no gap at all between them. Not even enough to be able to slip in a straight pin.

He was kissing her and she was kissing him.

And after the surprise of that came an even greater surprise: his reaction to that entirely unplanned, unexpected event.

He wanted to keep on kissing her.

Not just keep on kissing her but he wanted to deepen that kiss until there was nothing of any consequence left beyond its heated boundaries.

He wanted to take her breath away because she had taken the very air out of his world, leaving him winded—and wanting more.

Had she slipped something into his coffee to make him feel like this? Or was he just that deprived, that isolated?

For the life of him, he didn't know.

Code Red! Code Red!

His mind fairly shouted the alarm. In hospital-speak it meant that a fire was occurring in the facility—in this case inside of *him*—and it called for emergency measures to be taken immediately in order to ensure survival.

Which meant that if he intended to survive longer than the next couple of minutes, he was going to have to terminate contact.

Now.

Taking hold of Melanie's slim shoulders—the woman felt far more delicate than he knew she was—he pushed her back, away from him while silently and simultaneously mourning the immediate loss of contact.

He could have sworn he still tasted her on his lips. Blueberries. How the hell did he taste blueberries lingering on his lips when she'd been drinking coffee, same as he?

It didn't make sense. None of it made sense.

Especially not his kissing her. He had so much more restraint than that. Or at least he had, until now.

"Thanks for the coffee," he murmured, leaving the travel mug behind on the exam table. Clearing his throat, he told her, "Maybe next time it should have less of a kick."

"Maybe," Melanie heard herself say.

Or maybe she just *thought* she made a reply. The truth of it was, she was utterly stunned and more than a little dazed by what had just happened.

He'd kissed her.

Just like that, out of the blue.

She would have bet a million dollars—if she'd *had* a million dollars—that Mitch would have never even *considered* kissing her, much less doing it. And yet that was exactly what he'd done.

Her mind reeling, she tried to take stock and center herself. What had just happened here? And *why*? Was the world ending? Had something happened when she wasn't paying attention and they all had barely five minutes to live?

What other explanation *was* there? Sure, they'd

made eye contact on a few occasions, but that was a long way from *lip* contact, even if she'd felt something unsettling going on each time she was around him.

Get a grip, Mel, she ordered herself. *Stop making such a big deal about it. It was just a kiss, less than nothing. People do it all the time.*

Well, maybe *people* did it all the time, but *she* didn't. Ever.

She hadn't kissed another man, not since she was back in high school.

Jeremy had *always* been the one, there had never been any doubt in her mind. And now that he was no longer part of this life, well, she wasn't interested in making another connection with the male of the species, not in *that* way at any rate.

Oh yeah? So who was that I saw kissing Dr. Forget-Me-Not just now?

Closing her eyes for a moment, Melanie sighed. She had no answer for the taunting voice in her head. No theory to put forth to satisfy her conscience and this sudden, unannounced wave of guilt that had just washed over her. She wasn't even sure if the ground beneath her feet hadn't disappeared altogether. She felt just that unsteady.

She'd stayed sitting down even after Mitch had left the room.

Damn it, the man kissed you, he didn't perform a lobotomy on you with his tongue. Get a grip and get back to work. Life goes on, remember?

That was just the problem. Life went on. The love of her life had been taken away ten months ago and for some reason, life still went on.

Squaring her shoulders, she slid off the makeshift

exam table, otherwise known in her mind as the scene
of the crime, tested the steadiness of her legs and once
that was established, left the room.

Whether Melanie liked it or not, there was still a
lot of work to do and it wouldn't get done by itself.

She had almost managed to talk herself into a neu-
tral, rational place as she made her way past the dining hall which, when Mitch was here, still served as
his unofficial waiting room. That was when she heard
Mitch call out to her.

"Melanie, I need you."

Everything inside of her completely froze.

It was the same outside. It was as if her legs, after
working fine all these years, had suddenly forgotten
how to move and take her from point A to point B.

She had to have heard him wrong.

The Dr. Mitchell Stewart she had come to know
these past few weeks would have never uttered those
words to anyone, least of all to her.

*And would the Mitchell Stewart you think you know
so well have singed off your lips like that?*

Okay, so maybe she didn't know him as well as
she thought she did, but still, he wouldn't have said
something like that to her, especially where someone else—*anyone* else—could have heard him say it.

Knowing she couldn't afford to just ignore him
and keep on walking, Melanie blinked and turned her
head in his direction. She could feel her heart pounding like a jackhammer set on high.

"Excuse me?" she said in a raspy whisper, unable
to produce anything louder out of her mouth at the
moment no matter how hard she tried.

Was it her imagination, or was Mitch even sterner-looking right now than he had been at any other given time since she'd first met him?

"I've got to examine Mrs. Sanchez and Ms. Ames," he told her matter-of-factly, indicating the two women who were standing behind him. "I need to have another woman present. Regulations," he specified, looking no happier about having to ask her than she was to be asked. "Remember?"

"Oh." Of course, how could she have been so stupid? He wasn't telling her he needed her, he was telling her he *needed* her. "Yes. Of course," she answered in a stilted voice, feeling like an idiot. "Ready when you are, Doctor."

The problem was, Mitch thought as he walked past her to lead the way back to the makeshift exam room—the room where he had taken leave of his senses—he wasn't ready at all.

Volunteering was *definitely* not working out the way he had been led to believe that it would. He needed to rethink a few things the first chance he got, Mitch promised himself.

"You look feverish, Melanie. Are you all right?" Theresa asked, peering at the younger woman's face.

Concerned, the caterer walked away from the long tables where some of the people she'd brought with her were setting up, preparing to feed the shelter's residents the tenderloin stew that she had whipped up in her catering kitchen before coming here.

She paused now in front of Melanie and studied her a little more closely.

"I'm fine," Melanie protested, turning away self-consciously.

Even so, Theresa politely but firmly got in her way. Then, placing one hand on her shoulder to keep the younger woman from leaving, Theresa first touched the back of her hand to Melanie's forehead, then fell back on the universal Mother's Thermometer—she pressed her lips to Melanie's forehead.

"I don't know," Theresa said thoughtfully. "Your forehead seems a little warm to me."

Melanie supposed she should be grateful that the woman hadn't attempted to take her pulse. It was still doing a drumroll more than an hour after the fact. Mitch might very well have healing hands, but at the same time, the man had a lethal mouth.

"I've been running around," Melanie said evasively, doing her best to dismiss the other woman's less than scientific findings.

"Are you sure that's all it is? With everyone being in such close quarters here and all the little ones always coming down with colds, it's all too easy to catch something." She looked at Melanie knowingly. "Especially if you let yourself get run down."

"I'll keep that in mind," Melanie promised, trying her best to politely disentangle herself from the woman and get away before there were any more questions, ones that could trip her up.

And then, the very next minute, that was exactly what happened. "Maybe you should have Dr. Mitch check you out, just to be sure," Theresa suggested.

Melanie reacted before she could think to censor herself.

"No! I mean, no," she said, uttering the word several decibels lower, "the doctor's busy enough as it is seeing sick people. He doesn't have time to waste on someone with imaginary symptoms."

"Symptoms?" Theresa repeated with interest. "You didn't mention symptoms. What sort of symptoms are you experiencing?"

Flustered, Melanie tried to remember what the woman had said to her initially. "What you told me— that I looked flushed."

"I said feverish," Theresa gently corrected, looking not unlike an elementary school teacher catching one of her favorite students in a lie.

"Right. Feverish," Melanie repeated. "I meant feverish."

And she was getting more so by the second, Melanie couldn't help thinking. She was beginning to feel like a trapped hummingbird, desperately searching for an avenue of escape.

And getting nowhere.

Fast.

Taking Melanie's hand in hers, Theresa gently tugged on it as she deliberately moved farther away from the dining area and its ensuing noise.

Once she felt they had secured more privacy, Theresa fixed the younger woman with a compassionate look. "Tell me what's wrong, Melanie."

"Nothing's wrong," Melanie insisted.

She did her best to avoid the other woman's eyes. It was hard enough avoiding the truth without having to do it while making eye contact, as well. Theresa's eyes seemed to bore into her very soul.

And obviously, she discovered a moment later, she wasn't very successful at avoiding making eye contact.

"Melanie, I've raised two children and been around

a lot more in my time. Please believe me that I mean this in the nicest possible way, but you don't lie very well at all. Now please, be honest," Theresa implored. "Why do you suddenly look like a deer caught out in the open on the first day of hunting season?"

Melanie wanted to tell the woman that it was just her imagination. That there was nothing wrong and that she was most certainly *not* lying.

But she *was* lying and furthermore, she knew that she had no gift for it. To insist otherwise to Theresa would be insulting someone she liked as well as painting herself in a very bad light. Which was what she told her.

Or tried to.

"I—we—this is, he—he kissed me," Melanie finally managed to get out. To her ear, her own words sounded almost garbled.

"He?" Theresa asked, praying she wasn't jumping to conclusions. The last time she'd observed him—from a distance—while he was working, the exceptionally handsome doctor with the chiseled features behaved as if he had a heart to match…it was just under lock and key.

But keys could be used to open locks.

"Dr. Mitch." Melanie had to practically force the words out of her mouth.

"Oh, *he*," Theresa said, more pleased than she could remember being in a long, long time. "That he," she added just for good measure. And then she looked at Melanie a little more closely still. The young woman was obviously distressed. Disappointment descended over her like dark, heavy humidity from a hovering rain cloud.

"Was he that bad, dear?" she asked.

Guilt was pricking at her conscience since she was partially responsible for having orchestrated what was beginning to appear to be a disaster.

"No," Melanie replied, her voice sounding even more sorrowful than before, "he was that good."

Theresa's eyebrows knitted together in apparent complete confusion. Putting her arm around Melanie's shoulders, Theresa drew her even farther away from the dining area to an alcove that despite its rather open appearance, was still off to the side and away from general traffic.

"Forgive me for saying this, but at least in my day, when a young man kissed well, it was a thing to celebrate, however quietly, not bemoan," she added knowingly. "You look as if someone had just told you that a flash flood was imminent and then they tied lead weights to your ankles."

She might as well tell the woman the whole story so Theresa could at least understand why she was acting so upset.

"He kisses better than anything I've ever experienced," Melanie reluctantly admitted. "It's just that…" She knew she had to seem stupid to the other woman. "It's just that…"

Her voice trailed off. Melanie just couldn't bring herself to finish her sentence.

So Theresa finished it for her. "It's just that you feel disloyal to your late fiancé because you're feeling this way."

"Yes!" The word rushed out on its own power and once it was out, Melanie was almost relieved. But she wasn't accustomed to being so open about her feelings. "I mean, no."

"Do you?" Theresa gave her a penetrating look.

"No." Melanie sighed. Against her will, she told Theresa the reason behind her reaction. "That part of my life is over. I don't want to feel anything for another man."

Theresa was nothing if not understanding. She knew exactly what Melanie was experiencing—and she knew exactly why that was wrong at this stage of her life.

"Dear, you're young with your whole life ahead of you. You're not dead and Jeremy wouldn't have wanted you to behave as if you were," she argued.

Melanie stared at her, stunned. Not only had the woman hit it exactly on the head, she had also called her fiancé by his name. A name she had never mentioned to Theresa.

"How did you…?"

Theresa's smile effectively swept the pending question under the rug, to be disposed of at a later, more convenient date. Right now she needed to keep Melanie and the good doctor together.

"I have friends with connections," she told Melanie. "I ask questions about people I care about." She smiled at her. "You are a very good person, Melanie. You're selfless and you're always giving of yourself. Tell you what," she proposed, lowering her voice as if the two of them were planning some sort of necessary, secret invasion. "Why don't you do this? Why don't you give yourself permission to be happy? After all the good you've done here, you deserve to get a little happiness in return."

She gave Melanie a quick squeeze to seal the suggestion.

It was getting closer to dinnertime and Theresa knew she had to be getting back to oversee things. Her crew, as well as the regular volunteers here, were perfectly capable of handling things on their own, but she liked to think that she helped facilitate things a little.

"Trust me. I'm older. I'm right about this," the woman added with a wink. "And by the way, I intend to follow up on this, so get back to me," she instructed Melanie.

Melanie had no doubts that Theresa meant what she said about following up. Which was why the butterflies began dive-bombing with a vengeance in the pit of her stomach.

Chapter Eight

Thanks to several new people who had come to the shelter since his last visit, the rest of Mitch's afternoon was, for the most part, one new patient after another. The time was completely taken up with exams. So much so that despite the fact that he was working beside Melanie, no words were exchanged between them other than the necessary ones involving the patients.

It seemed like an endless shuffle of people with a few of the established patients mixed in. No sooner did one patient exit the tiny makeshift exam room than another entered, leaving absolutely no time for idle chatter, much less an awkwardly tendered apology on his part.

Mitch still wasn't sure if he had initiated what had happened between them, but if he'd learned one thing from listening to others talk, it was always the man's fault. It was far easier to accept blame than to contest it.

And easier still if he bowed out from the shelter altogether, he couldn't help thinking as he went home that evening. Under ordinary circumstances, he would have withdrawn his participation in the volunteer program without any qualms. But something had changed his perspective in the past few weeks. He'd always been a conscientious doctor in general. After coming here sometimes several times a week, he had, almost without actually realizing it, developed a sense of responsibility toward these people.

As a general surgeon, he rarely saw patients more than three, sometimes four times. Pre- and post-op, and of course, the day of the surgery. Once in a rare while, there were two post-op visits. Terminating his association with the shelter would leave the residents at the shelter in a bad way, at least temporarily. He knew he wouldn't feel right about it unless he found someone to take his place. So that had to become his next order of business.

It might be the next order of business but that didn't mean that it was going to be easy for him. He didn't interact with the other physicians at his hospital in that kind of manner. While he was always up for consultations and was ready with a second opinion if asked, Mitch didn't really socialize. He no longer attended hospital fund raisers and he didn't attend any smaller, more private parties. He didn't go out after a shift for a friendly drink. He didn't even go out for lunch with any of them, preferring to eat alone while he caught up on whatever else might need his attention at the time. He was accustomed to multitasking, not maintaining interpersonal relationships.

So how would he go about finding out if anyone would be willing to take his place at the shelter? Mitch wondered. And yet, if he wanted to ease himself out of the arrangement he'd made with the shelter, that was exactly what he was going to have to do.

He still hadn't come up with a solution by his next visit to the shelter. Abhorring awkward encounters, he decided to grab the bull by its proverbial horns and sought Melanie out before getting started with the scheduled exams for the afternoon.

But Melanie didn't seem to be around. It figured, he thought, getting his lab coat out of the closet. At the hospital, he tended to wear suits when consulting with patients and scrubs when operating on them. Here, the director had told him, the sight of a lab coat inspired a feeling of well-being. Though he believed it silly, he went along with it anyway.

"We need to talk," Melanie said, seemingly materializing out of thin air as she came up behind him.

Startled, he swung around. Damn, but she moved quietly. He didn't like being caught off guard. The next moment, he managed to collect himself.

Mitch crisply told her, "No, we don't." He'd just passed several women who'd said they needed to see him about one matter or another, and this convinced him that this wasn't the time or place to discuss his momentary lapse of judgment.

"Yes, we do," Melanie insisted.

She had spent the past two days agonizing over this moment. Despite her conversation with Theresa, she'd decided that she needed to nip this—whatever "this" turned out to be—in the bud. She didn't want that kiss, fantastic though it was, to lead to anything else between them—or to have him think that she expected it to lead to something else. She wanted it to be perfectly clear that she didn't *want* it leading to something else.

Ever.

"Look, if this is about the other day in the exam room—"

"It is," she interjected.

"Then there's no need to talk about it," he told her firmly.

Just as firmly, she said, "I disagree."

"Why doesn't that surprise me?" he asked, more of himself than of her. Thoughts about being chivalrous and accepting the blame evaporated. He just wanted her to agree to stop talking about it until another, more suitable time. "Look—"

She was sure that he was probably accustomed to charming his way through everything. He was handsome, he was successful in his field and undoubtedly used to winning, but she was not about to have him believing that there was a casual fling in the offing. There *was* no fling about to be flung, casual or otherwise.

"No, *you* look," she retorted forcefully. "I want to go on working here—I *need* to go on working here," she emphasized with feeling. "And the shelter definitely needs you to continue volunteering your time here. That's not going to work out if we're feeling self-conscious around one another—and *that's* not going to go away until we clear the air about expectations."

"Melanie," he began, trying to get in a word edgewise to let her know that he didn't have any expectations and if she did, well then he was very sorry about that but he in no way wanted her to believe that he was about to come through in that department, no matter *what* her expectations were.

But Melanie continued as if he hadn't made any attempt to curtail the conversation, hadn't said anything at all.

"There can't be any expectations," she informed him quietly.

The rebuttal he was forming in his mind came to an abrupt, skidding halt. Mitch stared at her, stunned. "What?"

"No expectations," she repeated. "I'm sorry if it seemed as if I was open to something happening between us, but I'm not and I don't want you worrying that this was going to blow up somewhere along the line because there isn't going to be anything to blow up. If I gave you the impression that there was going to be anything like that, that there was something between us, I'm really very sorry."

Listening to her, Mitch was both relieved—and just a little puzzled. Melanie was saying exactly what he had hoped for—that the moment of indulgence carried no consequences with it. He should have been pleased and immensely thankful.

And yet…

And yet he couldn't help being puzzled as to what would have prompted her to say something like that. Was there something about him that she found offputting? Yet, ultimately this was what he wanted—

so why did he find it so disturbing that she was, in essence, rejecting him?

He was pushing himself too hard. This was what happened when he overextended himself. He started making no sense at all.

"It's fine," he told her in a tone that said just the opposite.

It prompted her concern. Guilt, Melanie had discovered, was never very far away these days. She'd hurt his feelings or his ego, she wasn't sure which. Possibly both and she hadn't wanted to do either. She took another stab at an explanation and trying to make things right.

"It was a moment of weakness and I'm not sure why it happened, all I know is that I don't want anything like that in my life anymore." This was coming out all wrong. "I mean—"

"Anymore?"

That had been an unfortunate slip of the tongue, Melanie silently upbraided herself. At this point, she felt that the more she talked, the worse it was going to get.

"Never mind," Melanie said with finality, hoping to bury the subject altogether. "You have a lot of patients to see."

So now she was telling him his job? "I am aware of that," he retorted coolly.

"Good, then we're on the same page."

Not hardly, Mitch thought as he finally put on the white lab coat he'd gotten out of the closet what seemed like eons ago.

He had no time to wonder about what Melanie had said because the moment he slipped on his lab coat, there was a quick knock on the door frame and his first patient came in.

By now, he was familiar with all their faces, if not their names. But this patient was even more familiar than the others. The first patient of his afternoon was April O'Neill.

Seeing her, Mitch caught himself smiling almost automatically. There was something almost infectious about the little girl's wide, guileless smile and her entire manner was comprised of exuberance, despite the circumstances that she and her mother and brother found themselves in.

Hers was the face of eternal hope.

"Where's your mother?" Mitch asked. Ordinarily, mothers accompanied their children when they were brought in for an exam.

"She's busy with Jimmy," April told him matter-of-factly, as if this was just the way things were. She was the healthy one and her brother was not, which meant that he required more of their mother's time.

April willingly occupied herself at the shelter. She was a pint-size goodwill ambassador, wheedling information out of everyone and becoming part of the main fabric of the shelter in an extraordinarily short amount of time.

"Okay, well, you know the drill," Mitch told her, patting the top of the exam table. "Get up on the table and tell me where it hurts."

He was surprised when his small patient giggled in response, then watched as she scampered onto the exam table. He knew better than to help her up. April was exceedingly independent and proud of it.

This afternoon her progress was hampered because

she was holding a folder in her hand. Mitch assumed that the folder probably contained a note from the girl's mother, explaining the symptoms that had sent April to him in the first place.

"Okay," Mitch said, putting his stethoscope around his neck, "what brings you here?"

"My feet," April answered, looking up at him a little uncertainly because he had to ask. To emphasize her point, she wiggled them.

"No, I think the doctor wants to know why you came to see him this morning," Melanie explained.

"Oh." As understanding washed over her, April nodded her head vigorously. "Okay." Taking a deep breath, she went into her explanation. "I came to see him because I have something to give him. And you," she quickly added, looking at Melanie. Indicating the folder, April proudly declared, "This."

Then, unable to contain herself, April opened the folder before Melanie could reach for it.

Inside the folder were two pieces of eight-by-ten beige construction paper. Both had colorful drawings on them vividly immortalized with a number of different crayons. Below each of the drawings was a swarm of *X*s and *O*s. Beneath *that* someone had obviously helped April print her name in big block letters that seemed to lean into one another. The five letters were all inside of a huge red heart.

April's eyes danced as she held out her handiwork to both of them.

"Do you like it?" she asked eagerly, although from her tone of voice it was easy to see that she thought the answer was a foregone conclusion.

"Oh, very much," Melanie told her enthusiastically.

Holding it between both hands, Melanie held the drawing out as if she was appraising it.

"And you'll keep it forever?" April asked.

"And ever and ever," Melanie assured her with feeling.

April turned her huge bright green eyes on Mitch. "How about you?" she asked hopefully. "Do you like your card, Dr. Mitch?"

"It's very nice," Mitch replied. In his opinion, there was nothing special about it, but the little girl had made an effort and he'd been raised to believe that efforts were to be praised and rewarded if they were to yield something greater in turn. "But what's the card for?"

April cocked her head and looked at him as if she thought he was teasing her.

"Why, it's for Valentine's Day, silly. Today is Valentine's Day and I drew you Valentine cards 'cause you're both my Valentines. Mama thinks it's silly to give out cards, but I think everyone should have a Valentine card. We got some big paper from Mrs. Miller today at school. She told us to make a card for someone who we thought wasn't gonna get one. I asked her if I could make two so then she gave me two pieces of paper," April concluded, running out of breath at the end of her narrative.

She punctuated her story with a huge, sunny smile. But her smile quickly faded away when she look at Melanie. There were tears in Melanie's eyes.

"Don't you like your card?" April asked her, disappointed.

Melanie pressed her lips together, not trusting her

voice for a moment. Instead, because April was looking at her intently, she nodded her head.

"Very much," she finally ventured in a soft voice
that was almost a whisper.

"But your eyes are leaking again," April pointed
out. "Just like the last time."

"Those are happy tears, remember?" Melanie managed to get out. "Because the card you drew for me
is so beautiful."

"Oh. Okay." April brightened, accepting the excuse. Her cards delivered, the little girl wiggled down
off the table. "Well, that's all. I'm not really sick," she
confided as an afterthought. "I just wanted to come
and give you those cards I made for you 'cause it's
Valentine's Day."

With that, the little girl grabbed her folder and
darted out of the room.

Melanie turned toward the wall, as if desperately
trying to collect herself before the next patient walked
into the room.

Debating for a moment, Mitch made up his mind
and closed the door before anyone could enter. He
thought it best to give Melanie a moment before she
had to get back to work.

As he eased the door closed, he told himself he
wasn't going to say anything, that whatever was going
on with Melanie was her own business and in her
place, he wouldn't have appreciated being on the re-
ceiving end of any questions, however well intentioned
they might have been.

Despite this new self-awareness, Mitch heard himself asking her a question. His need to know had gotten the better of him.

"Why are your eyes 'leaking'?" he asked.

Hearing the six-foot-two, stern-faced doctor using April's term for crying caused her to smile. At least just enough to help her push back the dreadful wave of sorrow that had suddenly threatened to swallow her up whole.

"Because it's Valentine's Day."

"Do you always cry on Valentine's Day?" he asked.

He kept his voice mild, thinking that might just coax a response out of her. If he asked point-blank in his usual brusque manner, he knew she'd just close up and make it impossible for him to find out anything.

But maybe having this conversation would bring her around enough to be able to at least face working for the rest of the day.

"Is this something like when Charlie Brown stands by his mailbox and sighs because his dog gets a ton of Valentine cards while he doesn't get any?" he asked when she didn't answer him.

Brushing aside her tears with the heel of her hand, Melanie turned around and looked at the man before her in amazement.

"You've actually read a comic strip?"

"I have," he corrected. "As a kid." It had been years since he'd even glanced at a comic strip. Maybe he should make a point of finding a newspaper and catching up a bit, just for old time's sake, he thought whimsically. Out loud he said matter-of-factly, "Some things stick in your head."

"I guess," Melanie allowed. And then, because he was trying to be helpful—at least for him—she decided that maybe she owed him a little bit more of an explanation than she'd given him. "I completely forgot today was Valentine's Day."

That was no big deal. Certainly not something to cry over. "You're not alone," he assured her.

But Melanie shook her head. "No, you don't understand."

"So you keep telling me," he remarked with a patient sigh.

Melanie drew in a long breath and decided she might as well get the whole thing out rather than harbor it like some deep, dark secret. Secrets usually wound up festering. Besides, it wasn't as if she was ashamed of what she had done or of Jeremy.

"I got engaged on Valentine's Day."

The name of her fiancé escaped him at the moment. He sought for a way to tactfully work his way around that deficit without calling attention to it. "To the man who never came home."

She felt fresh tears threatening to descend. How could she have forgotten that today was Valentine's Day? "Yes, to him."

"Look, if you want to go home, I can have the director find someone else to—"

"No," Melanie said firmly, cutting him off. She knew what he was going to say and she didn't want to hear it. "I don't want to go home. I want to be right here, where I can at least be useful to someone for something. I'll call your next patient in," she said abruptly, striding past him.

He saw no reason to try to stop her. By now he'd learned that he couldn't, even if he tried.

Chapter Nine

"You're good with them."

Mitch made the observation half grudgingly in the exam room several days after April had presented them with her hand-drawn Valentine cards. It was the tail end of the day and as usual, a swarm of children had been herded through the makeshift exam room.

But, unlike usual, the swarm of children had abruptly stopped.

He'd made the remark grudgingly because he *didn't* want to find anything more to admire about Melanie. Things would be a whole lot better for him if he could simply just not notice her at all. But that was like trying not to notice a clear summer day, or a crisp warm breeze on a spring morning.

The truth was he couldn't *help* noticing her and the way the children here not just reacted to her but gravitated to her, as well. It was as if she were this beguiling, all-encompassing magnet and the children were metal filings who instantly were attracted to her the moment they found themselves with her.

He had a set way of doing things, a way of expecting certain results after certain things were done. She, on the other hand, appeared to be as flexible as a licorice whip—physically, if he was any judge, watching her—as well as emotionally.

He had no doubts that if Melanie weren't here, acting as his go-between with the children each time he came to the shelter to minister to them, he would have had a great deal more trouble dealing with his small patients. For the most part, they were lively and exuberant, but they still seemed to *want* to behave for her, which completely amazed him.

Melanie casually shrugged off the doctor's observation. "Most kids want to behave. They just need to be guided a little."

"I think it's more than that," he countered. "I think they want to please you."

And she, he'd noticed, always knew just how to respond to make them laugh and feel good. He didn't have that gift and, until just recently, hadn't even felt the lack of it. But working beside this woman, he'd become acutely aware of the fact that the connections he made with his patients were sorely insufficient. It bothered him that it bothered him—and yet, it did.

"Did you have a lot of brothers and sisters growing up?" he asked.

The way he saw it, that would have been a reason why Melanie could get along so well with children. He, on the other hand, had been an only child and had kept to himself for the most part, preferring his own company to that of the kids in the neighborhood. Consequently, his people skills—much less his ability to communicate with children—had never been honed.

"No, actually," she told him. "I didn't have any. But I remember what it was like."

"What *what* was like?" he asked, feeling as if he'd lost her.

"Being a kid," she explained. "I remember what it was like." It was right there, a vivid part of her, everything she'd ever experienced as a child. "How scary things seemed. I can relate to all that. Most of the time, there was just my mother and me," she told Mitch. "My dad was in the navy and we moved around a lot. Every time I turned around, I was the new kid on the block." She laughed quietly. It hadn't been easy. "That involved a lot of insecurity and a lot of adjusting on my part. I wound up getting a very broad education."

"You were an only child?" he asked.

It gave them something in common, and at the same time, they couldn't have been more different, Mitch thought. She was the very definition of open and outgoing and he could easily be an island unto himself.

Well, maybe not easily, he amended, looking at Melanie, but he still could be.

Melanie nodded. "There were years I would have killed for a brother or sister. Especially an older brother to look out for me when we lived in this one place that I swear was populated with nothing but these sharp-tongued 'mean girls.'" A rueful look passed over her face. "Eventually, I realized that siblings—older *or* younger—weren't coming."

She stiffened just a little, as if bracing herself against the memory of what she was about to say. "Then my dad met someone else and it was just my mom and me." And then she brightened a little. "That's when we settled down in Bedford and for the first time, my life actually became stable. I knew where I'd be from one month to the next. I got to go to the same high school for the whole four years—I felt like I'd died and gone to heaven," she enthused. "And for a while, I guess I had."

He watched as she got a faraway look in her eyes and for a moment, she seemed not even to be in the same room anymore.

"But then things changed," she went on to say matter-of-factly, her voice distant and emotionless. "My mom died, and then—" Melanie blinked, as if she was suddenly hearing herself. "How did I get started talking about this?"

Something akin to what he supposed passed for compassion stirred inside of him. "I remarked that you were good with kids and you took it from there."

Melanie cleared her throat as she shrugged dismissively. "Sorry, I didn't mean to bore you."

"You didn't," he told her.

And that made her feel even more self-conscious, as if she was somehow exposed and unable to hide anything. Although Melanie had no problem talking, she didn't usually talk about herself. Doing that made her feel vulnerable and there was nothing she hated more than that feeling.

Peering out into the dining area, she saw a few of the residents—the ones who weren't lucky enough to find some sort of part-time employment in the local shops in the area—milling around. But none of the women appeared to be waiting their turn with the doctor.

That was a first, she couldn't help thinking.

"Looks like you ran out of patients," she observed, turning around to face him again. "I guess that means you're free to go."

Mitch laughed shortly. "I suppose I am." He paused for a moment, silently debating the wisdom of the question hovering on his tongue. And then it stopped hovering and became a reality. "Do you want to go grab a cup of coffee somewhere?"

"There's coffee in the dining area," she pointed out, wondering how he had forgotten about that.

"I mean a *real* cup of coffee," Mitch emphasized.

"You mean one that costs too much?" She assumed that was probably his criteria—if it didn't cost a sinful amount, the product he was getting couldn't be any good.

The man was still a snob, she thought, but at least he seemed to be coming around.

"I mean one that doesn't taste like someone dipped a brown crayon in hot water for approximately three minutes."

"I'd take offense at that remark," she told him with a straight face—and then she smiled. "But I guess it is pretty weak at that," she admitted.

He was still processing the first part of her statement. "You make the coffee?" he asked. He hadn't meant to insult her, he just didn't associate making coffee as part of what she did at the shelter.

"Some of the time," Melanie admitted. "Coffee's

not much of a priority around here. There's more of an emphasis on milk and wholesome food—and a doctor's care," she added on for good measure. "You're the first doctor some of these women have had contact with since—well, forever, I guess." She looked at him for a moment, as if finally allowing herself to see him. "Frankly, I'm surprised you stuck around."

"That makes two of us," Mitch murmured under his breath.

His admission had her regarding him a little more closely. "Does that mean you might stop coming to the shelter soon?" she asked. It was always best to be braced than to stick her head in the sand. That had become her new motto.

As Mitch watched her, she squared her shoulders and seemed to shut down right in front of his eyes.

"If I did stop coming here, would that matter to you?" he wanted to know. He told himself he was just making conversation—but he actually wanted to know and the fact that he did bothered him. It shouldn't have mattered to him one way or another—but it did.

Melanie shifted the emphasis away from her. It was how she'd learned to survive.

"It would matter to the residents here—especially to the children like April. She's gotten very attached to you, Doctor. Children value a routine. They get used to it, depend on it. You take that routine away from them, you risk making their worlds collapse."

He didn't buy that. Was she trying to guilt him into staying because *she* didn't want him to stop coming—or was she just spinning a theory? He couldn't tell.

"As someone whose father was in the navy, you

know that changes are a part of life. It can happen at any time, any age," he pointed out.

She thought of how she had felt when she'd learned about Jeremy. How her whole world had completely shattered.

"Yes," she said quietly. "I know." And then she forced herself to rally. She didn't want him asking her any questions. "If you do decide that you've had enough of volunteering, I'd appreciate you letting me know before it becomes general knowledge. I'd like to be able to prepare the kids."

"I'm sure that it wouldn't really be that a big a deal for them," he told her dismissively.

Her eyes met his for a moment and he couldn't really begin to guess what she was thinking. "You'd be surprised," she told him quietly.

"Maybe," he allowed. And then he heard himself say something that left him wide open to a whole array of things that he had told himself he was trying to avoid. "When do you leave here?"

She didn't understand the question. "I'm sorry?"

I don't know about you, but I know I might be.

Still, Mitch knew he had to follow this thought through to the end. "In the evening, do you leave at a set time or whenever you want to, or…?" He allowed his voice to trail off, leaving her space to jump in any time.

"Probably more like 'or,'" she told him. When he looked at her questioningly, she elaborated. "There's no real set time. I usually leave when things settle down and the mothers who have jobs come back in time to eat with their kids, help them with their homework if the kids are old enough to attend one of the local schools. In a nutshell, I go home when I'm not needed."

"Oh." He looked at her. Mitch was beginning to think that she really was an amazing woman. "Then you pretty much stay here all the time."

His subtle response tickled her and she laughed. "Is that a compliment?"

"Did sound like one, didn't it?" Mitch seemed to marvel right along with her, turning his comment around to absorb it.

She was still examining his words from all angles, as if they were a rare Christmas gift. "I think that's the first compliment you've given me."

He didn't doubt it. He wasn't the type to be lavish with his praise. It was both his strength and his shortcoming, he thought.

"Probably."

"Any particular reason you're trying to pin me down to a schedule?" she asked him.

He might as well have it all out in the open, Mitch thought. "I guess I'm trying to ask you out to dinner."

"What happened to coffee?"

"Dinner's better," he told her.

Her mind was on expediency. "We could eat here in the dining hall."

"Or we could eat somewhere less crowded, where everyone wasn't watching our every move and counting the number of times we actually spoke to one another."

She would have loved to have gotten an updated tally on that, she thought. Melanie grinned for the first time that day.

"I guess you might have a point."

"I *always* have a point," he told her with total conviction. Then, realizing that he sounded rather stiff and formal, he did his best to lighten up a little. "So, when *are* you free?"

She glanced at her watch. It was a little past four. Barring an emergency, things would be winding down for the day very soon. Half an hour, tops. She could be ready to leave in half an hour.

Tell him no. You don't want to set yourself up, Mel. Been there, done that, remember? Make the right choice. Say no.

She took a deep breath, very aware of the mini-war going on inside her. "I'll have to get back to you about that," she told him.

"Sure," he told. "That's fine. Whenever."

Maybe this was for the best. He didn't want to start something that he might wind up regretting. Relationships were draining—or so he'd heard.

He knew his mother would have loved to have a daughter-in-law, grandchildren—the whole nine yards. But that wasn't his dream. He just wanted to continue doing what he'd been doing—being a doctor who made a difference.

Any other words they might have wanted to exchange on the subject were quickly tabled when they heard someone shouting in a loud, angry voice that threatened to haunt some of the younger children's nightmares for several months or more.

"I said, *Where is she?* I know she's here so *tell me* if you know what's good for you!"

By the sound of it, the man's fury seemed to increase with every word.

Before he had a chance to ask Melanie if she had

any idea what was going on, she'd taken off for the front of the shelter, where the voice was coming from.

He was right behind her and got to the main entrance at the same time that she did. The man doing the shouting was there, screaming and berating the shelter's director. To her credit, Polly appeared steadfast and unfazed, despite the man's considerable height and girth.

In his mid to late forties, the angry man was muscular and formidable looking. He also seemed as if he was the type who could beat anyone to a pulp who had the nerve to get in his way. At the moment, he was towering menacingly over the director.

Polly was standing her ground but it was anyone's guess for how long.

"If you're going to behave this way, I'm afraid you're going to have to leave. You're scaring the children," Polly told the man just as Melanie and he entered.

"Oh, like I give a damn about them," he snorted. Going toe-to-toe with Polly, he went on to rant, "I'll leave. Sure, I'll leave—*as soon as I find that whore and my kid!*" He started to push Polly aside.

"You get away from her!" Melanie shouted at him, rushing to get between the man and Polly.

Mitch snapped to attention, realizing that Melanie was going to try to shield the director from the man's ham-like fists.

Was she out of her mind?

Grabbing Melanie by the arm, he pulled her back and then rather than getting in front of her, he put himself in front of the angry man.

"Looks like it's unanimous," Mitch told him in a

calm voice that belied what was going on inside of him. "The ladies would like you to leave."

"Like I give a damn what the hell they want," the man spat. "What about you, tough guy? You want me to leave, too?" the man sneered at Mitch.

"Please, leave. We don't want any trouble," Polly was pleading, but neither man was listening. Like two lions, they sized one another up.

"I think it would be a good idea, yes," Mitch told the other man, never taking his eyes off him.

"Oh, you do, do you?" the man jeered. "Well, the hell with what you think and the hell with you!" he raged. Pulling back his right forearm, he fisted his hand and was about to throw a punch that threatened to bring the verbal exchange between them to a quick, painful end.

And it might have, if he had been able to follow through with that punch and connect with his intended target.

But to his stunned surprise, the man he obviously looked upon as an easy knockout turned out to be faster than he was.

Faster, more accurate and, as it turned out, had a one-two punch that was far more lethal than he'd counted on.

The first punch landed in the man's solar plexus, the second went straight to his jaw. The lumbering hulk was facedown on the floor in a matter of seconds without having landed so much as a single punch.

Taking no chances, Mitch kept a wary eye on the unconscious, would-be assailant. "Call 911," he told Polly, raising his voice to be heard above a chorus of childish cheers.

The children seemed to have materialized out of nowhere, descending upon the tight circle of angry men like invading locusts, just in time to have witnessed Mitch reduce the irrational assailant to a lump of inert—for now—flesh. The children, drawn by the shouting, had seen the rather quiet doctor who gave them pain-free shots behave like a hero and save Miss Polly—and maybe them, as well—because despite their tender ages, they had all seen that sort of craziness in their short lifetimes and they knew enough to get as far away from the unconscious man as possible.

"Already doing it."

The response came from Melanie, who had her cell phone out and against her ear. Covering the other ear, she turned away the second she heard her call being answered on the other end.

To everyone's relief, the police arrived quickly. The assailant, who turned out to be the ex-boyfriend of one of the shelter's new residents, was still out cold and thus offered no resistance when he was handcuffed and carried off to the patrol car.

Statements were taken down quickly. Since the assailant had taken the first swing—as well as having threatened Polly—he was brought down to the precinct to be booked for assault and disorderly conduct among other charges.

Melanie had held her breath throughout most of the ordeal. She waited until the arresting officers had left with their semiconscious prisoner and Polly had voiced her thanks, which Mitch, in typical fashion, had brushed aside.

Melanie also waited until the children—excited

by the act of heroism they had witnessed—had been herded off, as well.

Eventually, after enough time had passed and the activity had wound down, it was just the two of them standing alone in the foyer.

Aware of the fact that she had remained standing at his side during the entire time, Mitch looked at her now and read between the lines—or tried to.

"Well, say it," he urged. "Get it off your chest. You're obviously waiting to say something to me."

He had a feeling that Melanie was probably one of those women who hated physical fighting for any reason.

"Your knuckles are bruised," Melanie finally told him.

He looked at her, stunned. "That's it?" he asked in disbelief.

"No." She took him by the hand—gently—and began to lead him back to the exam room. "You need someone to take care of that for you. I've watched you work long enough to be the one to do that for you."

"I just have to wash my hands," he said, dismissing her concern.

The way he saw it, the condition of his knuckles didn't need any sort of attention or special treatment to be dispensed. Just some clean soap and water, and maybe a little time.

"No, you need to have that wound disinfected. I wouldn't doubt that that man has rabies. At any rate, you can never be too careful." She stopped to give him what amounted to a stern look. "Physician, heal thyself," she instructed firmly.

"I don't need anyone hovering over me. I can 'heal' myself," he insisted.

Melanie slanted a silencing glare in his direction. "Maybe, but I can do it better."

With that, she continued to lead him back to the exam room, steering him and taking charge as if he were a willful child who needed to be cared for.

Chapter Ten

Mitch was beginning to realize that the only way he was going to be able to leave the shelter with a minimum of difficulty was if he just gave in and allowed Melanie to see to the abrasions and bruises on his knuckles. So he allowed her to lead him into the very same room where he normally treated the shelter's residents.

"Take a seat," Melanie said, indicating the exam table.

He slid onto it. "I know the drill."

As she took out the necessary items, Melanie flashed a smile at him in response. "Good."

He sat there, watching her work, and Mitch had to admit that he was surprised at her efficiency. Obviously the woman had been paying more attention than he thought she had these past few weeks.

Melanie moved quickly and competently, disinfecting the two cuts across his knuckles. One of them went a lot deeper than he'd realized. The sharp sting surprised him and he'd almost winced, but managed to catch himself at the last moment.

Once she'd gotten the cuts cleaned, she liberally applied a salve to both areas and then covered them with two flexible bandages. Both had cartoon squirrels on them.

"Sorry about that," she apologized as she secured each one at a time. "We seem to be out of regular bandages."

The corners of his mouth curved ever so slightly in amusement as he regarded the end results. "Not bad," he pronounced.

"I told you I've been paying attention," she reminded him. After putting the items back into the first aid kit, Melanie closed the lid and set the kit back into the cabinet where it belonged. Locking it, she turned toward him and said, "Okay."

"Okay?" Mitch repeated the word, puzzled. He had no idea what she had just agreed to. He would have guessed that she was telling him that he could go home, but the inflection in her voice didn't match that scenario. "Okay what?"

She shifted so that she was standing right in front of him as she gazed up into his eyes. For just a split second, the very vivid memory of his single transgression rose up like a hot wave, drenching him before it receded again.

"Okay," she told him, "I'll have dinner with you, Mitch."

Well, that had certainly come out of the blue, he thought. "When?"

"Now," she told him. "I just wanted to finish taking care of your hand." She regarded her handiwork for a moment. "I didn't know you were a southpaw." She'd seen him work, and he always used his right hand. But when he'd turned out that rude man's lights, he'd done it by using his left hand.

"I'm not. But the coach in high school got me to switch when I injured my right hand. Said that if I practiced using both hands, that gave me twice the staying power in the ring and that my opponents would never know what was coming." He shrugged at the distant memory. "At the time, it made sense to me. I enjoyed the release that boxing afforded me, so I went along with anything the coach said."

The man was just full of surprises, Melanie thought. "You *boxed* in high school?"

"Yes." He saw the expression of disbelief on her face. "Why do you look so surprised?"

She'd always maintained that people weren't two dimensional, that they were complicated. It was just that Mitch had seemed so aloof, she didn't see him as having any sort of physical contact with other students.

"I guess I shouldn't be, considering how much you like dealing with people," she told him with a laugh. Punching out someone's lights seemed to make sense in that context. Once she finished putting everything away, she turned around and declared, "There, all done."

"Will I live, 'Doctor'?"

Her eyes crinkled ever so slightly at the corners as she said, "I'm happy to say yes."

"Happy?" he questioned.

Melanie raised her eyes to his. The doctor's stock had gone up immeasurably in her estimation when he had come to Polly's rescue like that, without any prompting from anyone. Especially doing it the way he had.

If anything, she would have expected Mitch to attempt to talk the man down, at the very least talk him out of his rage. She was familiar enough with the type to know that words would be wasted in that instance, but she hadn't thought Mitch would be aware of that.

The bull of a man could have easily hurt Polly and anyone else who got in his way. Looking back, this was clearly a case of actions speaking louder than words and she was very, very impressed that Mitch had gotten the situation under control with a minimum of fuss.

She was also relieved that he had only sustained a couple of cuts on his hand. It could have gone a great deal worse.

Melanie smiled at the bemused expression on his face now.

"Yes, happy. It would be terrible if after saving Polly like that—not to mention that man's poor ex-girlfriend and his child—you'd succumb to some microbe that can't be seen by the naked eye."

He didn't bother pointing out that a microbe, by definition, couldn't be seen by the naked eye. He just accepted her display of concern.

"Wouldn't want that."

Something else occurred to her. "Just out of curiosity, are you up on your shots?"

"Why?" he asked, intrigued. "What did you have in mind?"

But she wasn't bantering right now. "Your tetanus shot," she specified in all seriousness.

Mitch shrugged. Things like that were a regular part of his life, but as to when, well that was another story. "I think so."

"You *think* so?" she questioned, surprised that he was so vague about it. "You're a doctor, aren't you supposed to know?"

"I'm a doctor, that makes me too busy to know," he pointed out. Her concern had been almost sweet, but now she was carrying this too far. "I'm sure it's in my records somewhere."

"Somewhere?" She wasn't about to let up. This could have serious implications if his booster was out of date. One hand on her hip, she got in his way just in case he got it into his head that he was fed up and just wanted to take off. "Find out where."

He should have gotten really annoyed by now and couldn't figure out why he hadn't. "You don't let up, do you?"

Melanie moved her head from side to side, never taking her eyes off his. "Uh-uh."

"Okay, I remember," he said glibly. "I've had my shots."

She eyed him suspiciously. "Not good enough. I don't believe you."

"Not my problem," he told her. But when he started for the door, Melanie moved right along with him, blocking his path every step of the way. Mitch stopped moving. "You really *are* serious about this." He was stunned that she could be so adamant about something that would seem so minor to most people.

"Totally." She was dogged about him remaining

well and didn't see that as something to be ashamed of. "Call your doctor, or the hospital since they have to have your medical records," she realized, "and just verify that you had a booster shot within the past ten years. You did a brave thing out there. I'm not going to let it all end badly because you're just too stubborn to check a simple fact."

The woman could definitely be a pain, he thought, though he still wondered why his indignation over this minidrama failed to take root.

With a sigh, he took out his cell phone and called the personnel director at Bedford Memorial. Fifteen minutes and two recorded menu choices later, he finally had a date to give the tenacious, blond-haired bulldog before him.

"Satisfied?" he asked after having rattled off the date.

Her intense expression faded. "Yes. I'm just being cautious," she told him, putting away the booster serum she'd taken out—just in case.

"That's one description for it," he murmured, still trying to summon a little righteous indignation. But the truth was, no one had ever expressed this much concern over his well-being except for his mother. It did make him see Melanie in a totally different light than his initial perception of her.

Finally free to leave, he surprised her by remaining where he was.

"You're not leaving," she noted, getting her own things together for a second time.

"We're having dinner together, remember? Before this little tetanus shot confrontation of yours, you said 'okay,' that you'd have dinner with me," he reminded her.

She'd thought that since she'd refused to back off about the infection, she'd gotten him too annoyed to want to go out for a meal with her.

"You still want to do that?" she questioned in surprise.

"I wouldn't be asking if I didn't," he pointed out. "Any place in particular you'd like to go?" he asked as he escorted her out of the exam room. He locked the door behind him.

"Some place where they serve food would be nice," she deadpanned.

He watched her warily, waiting for some sort of coda to follow, some condition she wanted him to fulfill, like a damsel asking a knight to slay a dragon for her before he came over to the castle.

"Uh-huh. And...?" he asked, waiting for a shoe to drop.

"And nothing," she answered cheerfully. That seemed to be enough to her. "I'm easy."

Mitch stared at her, and then he laughed shortly. "Not hardly. But you go right on telling yourself that and maybe someday that'll almost be true."

With that, he finally got her out the front door and heading in the direction of his car.

"So, how long did you box?" she asked him half an hour later over a plate of Yankee pot roast, mashed potatoes and green beans.

He didn't even have to pause and try to remember. "Not long."

"Afraid someone was going to ruin your pretty

face?" she asked, amused. Since all his features appeared to be perfect, she assumed his high school boxing venture was over before it ever got started.

"Afraid someone was going to ruin my pretty hands," he corrected. "I was still in high school when I decided I was going to be a surgeon." Or rather, when his father had made that decision for him, he recalled. "And that meant not risking breaking anything useful, like my fingers, or my wrist, or anything else in that vicinity."

When his father had found out that he was on the boxing team, he'd read him the riot act and made him quit that very afternoon. He remembered entertaining the idea of just rebelling, then, ever logical, he decided that his father was right and quit the team on his own.

"Makes sense," Melanie agreed. She could feel his eyes on her, as if he were trying to make up his mind about something. She made it easy for him and asked, "What?"

"What was that crack about my 'pretty face'?" he asked.

Her grin was utterly guileless in its delight. "I overheard some of the little girls talking. Seems that more than a few of them have a crush on you. The consensus is that you're even, and I quote, 'cuter than Ricky Harris.' That assessment, by the way, was followed by a chorus of squeals."

Mitch frowned as he tried to place the name. It meant nothing to him. "Who's Ricky Harris?"

Melanie feigned surprise. "You don't know?" And then she took pity on him and told him. "Ricky Harris is the preteen giant heartthrob of the moment. He has a couple of songs out right now and is the current big deal—until the next one comes along," she added, leaving the fact that it was a cutthroat business unsaid but completely understood.

The fact that she actually knew these miscellaneous details boggled his mind. "How do you keep up on all this?" he asked.

"I keep up on the kids and this is important to them, so I make it a point to keep up on who the current teen prince is."

Everything he had witnessed ever since he'd started volunteering at the shelter painted her to be good at what she was doing—in every aspect.

"Makes sense," he commented, then, before he could think his question through, he asked, "Why is it that you don't have any kids of your own?"

The light seemed to leave her face then. It took her another moment to pull herself together enough to answer his unintentionally hurtful question.

"Things just didn't arrange themselves that way," she told him quietly.

He heard the pain in every syllable. "Look, I'm sorry. I'm an idiot. I should have remembered," he could have kicked himself for that. "Or I shouldn't have asked at all. Or—"

He appeared genuinely miserable over upsetting her this way and that in itself helped her rally back to being her usual self, or at least the "self" she allowed the others to see. Otherwise, she was certain that all she would be doing all day was crying.

Melanie placed her hand on his and pressed it lightly. She was silently asking him to stop berating himself.

"It's okay," she told him. "You didn't mean anything by it. It was an honest mistake. And I do love kids." A very fond smile curved her lips. "Had things gone a different route, I might have one day wound up giving the old woman in a shoe a run for her money."

Mitch looked at her blankly, and then shook his head. "I'm sorry," he told her honestly, "I don't get the reference."

"The nursery rhyme," she prompted. "You never heard that nursery rhyme?" she asked in disbelief.

"I never heard *any* nursery rhyme," he told her. "My father believed that everything that was part of my upbringing should be goal oriented and my 'goal' was to be a doctor, a surgeon."

"Was that his idea, or yours?"

He thought of lying, but then he didn't see that there was anything to be gained by that. It didn't even buy him time because he wasn't in the market for it.

"His," he told her honestly.

That explained a lot, she thought. Still, that didn't begin to explain the gap in his knowledge. "Doctors know nursery rhymes."

Mitch shook his head. "Not in my father's world they don't."

Melanie thought of something else, something that her own childhood had been very rich in. She couldn't begin to imagine childhood without it.

"What about cartoons?" she asked.

"What about them?"

"Did you watch any?" she asked patiently.

He thought back for a moment. Some of his fondest memories were rooted in what she was asking about. "My mother snuck me out a few times when my father was away, attending conferences—he was always the main speaker when he attended," he added. "Don't get me wrong, I was proud to be his son. He was an excellent surgeon."

That alone didn't qualify to make the man a nominee for Father of the Year, Melanie couldn't help thinking. "Just not a warm and fuzzy father," she guessed.

"No," he admitted. To say otherwise would have been lying. "But he just wanted me to reach my full potential," he told her.

"Reading a few nursery rhymes wouldn't have prevented you from attaining that," she pointed out.

Mitch laughed, shaking his head. "I don't think he saw it quite that way. To him, watching cartoons or playing games was all pointless downtime."

Everyone needed to have a way to unwind, to be something outside the student, or the lawyer or the engineer.

"He must have been thrilled when he found out that you were on the boxing team," she guessed.

Mitch laughed drily before he could prevent it. "Who do you think pointed out how many different ways I could break my hand—not to mention that I could sustain some kind of brain damage from a blow to the head—which," he said, going back to her initial question, "would do a lot more damage than ruining my 'pretty face.'"

Melanie was quick to offer him a sympathetic smile. "We have a lot more in common than I thought," she commented.

He hadn't been aware that they were discussing their pasts. "What do you mean?"

She spelled it out for him without trying to sound

preachy. "Sounds like you had a rough childhood in your own way, too."

"I wouldn't exactly call it 'rough.' If anything I'd call it…isolated," he finally said, settling on a word.

"That's okay," she told him. "I'd call it rough for you." As she picked up her soda to take the last sip, she glanced at her watch. The time on it surprised her. "How did it get to be so late? You probably feel like I talked your ears off," she guessed ruefully.

Still looking at her, Mitch touched each of his ears one at a time.

"Nope, they're both still there," he informed her as if he'd just taken inventory of an actual shipment. "Better luck next time."

"Next time?" she repeated, confused. And maybe just a little bit nervous as well.

"Yes, I thought that since we're still both breathing and no mortal wounds have been delivered—"

He didn't get a chance to finish his sentence, or even to ask her out for a formal date. Anything he had to say on any subject was temporarily tabled as his cell phone began to ring.

The odd thing about that was hers did, as well. She had hers out first.

"It's the shelter," she told him, looking down at her phone's caller ID.

The caller ID on his cell phone was the same as hers. The shelter was calling both of them.

Chapter Eleven

Mitch had never believed in coincidences. Something was definitely wrong here.

Pressing Accept on his phone, Mitch said, "Dr. Stewart," at the same time that Melanie took her call and identified herself to her caller.

"Dr. Stewart, there's just been a horrific accident. I know this is a huge imposition, but are you anywhere close by and able to return to the shelter?"

The question throbbed with emotion. He barely recognized the shelter director's voice. He'd never heard her sound this beside herself or upset. Ordinarily, the woman seemed unflappable.

His first thought was that the man who had threatened to storm the homeless shelter earlier searching for his missing ex-wife and child had managed to make bail and was back.

Rather than speculate, Mitch asked. "Miss French, what happened?"

The director didn't seem to hear him. Instead, she was disjointedly rattling things off, giving him a summary of peripheral events rather than the main action.

"There's an ambulance on its way, but I know everyone here would feel a lot better if you could just please come back." She was literally begging now.

Mitch had a feeling that he wasn't going to have the blanks filled in by talking to the director. He would have to come back to the shelter and see what was going on for himself.

But what really made up his mind for him was the stricken expression on Melanie's face.

"On my way," he promised, closing his phone.

Melanie was doing the same. She forgot where she had put the phone the moment she had tucked it away. Her call had come from Theresa, who, it turned out, had decided to linger a while longer at the shelter tonight. The woman had just been on her way to her catering van when she saw the whole accident unfold.

It was the classic case of a speeding vehicle versus pedestrians.

Mitch immediately noticed that Melanie appeared very unsteady on her feet. He grabbed hold of her arm in case she passed out. He didn't want her possibly hitting her head. He didn't need another patient right now.

Taking out his wallet, he left two fifty-dollar bills on the table. He knew roughly what the meals had cost and he made sure that what he left behind more than covered the costs plus a generous tip. He absolutely didn't want to waste any time waiting for his credit card to be processed and returned for his signature. From the breathless way the director had begged him to come, he had a feeling that minutes might very well be of tantamount importance.

He looked at Melanie now as he ushered her out of the restaurant. The woman hadn't said a word since they had both terminated their calls, nor had she answered his question about the incident.

Had she gone into shock?

"Melanie?"

He stopped just short of where he'd parked his vehicle. Still holding on to her, this time with his hands bracketing both sides of her shoulders, he peered into her face.

"Are you all right?" he asked.

The sound of his voice managed to penetrate the deep fog around her brain. Coming to, she remembered the last thing he'd asked her. He wanted to know about the accident.

"A car hit them," she cried. "They were crossing the street, coming back from the playground and a hit-and-run driver plowed right into them and just kept going." Tears fell as she told him.

"Into who, Melanie?" he asked, repeating, "Into who?"

"April and her family," she answered in a stunned, stilted voice that didn't even sound real to her own ears. The very words tasted bitter.

"Let's go" was all she heard Mitch say.

The next moment, he was pushing her into the passenger seat of his car and closed the door. Rounding the hood, he threw himself into the driver's seat.

"Buckle up!" he ordered in a gruff voice, trying

his best to snap her out of this downward spiral she seemed to be slipping into. "C'mon, Melanie. Snap out of it. If it *is* them, that little girl is going to need you," he shouted at her.

This wasn't real. None of it seemed real. "What if…what if she's…dead?"

The word felt like a lead brick on her throat, threatening to choke her just the way it had when she'd stood there, listening to the kind-faced chaplain telling her life was over because Jeremy's life had been cut short.

"She's not dead," Mitch bit off angrily, revving up his engine. "Do you hear me? She's *not* dead."

Melanie looked at him as if seeing him for the first time since she'd taken the call. "You can't know that," she cried, fighting panic.

He made no answer because she was right. He couldn't know that.

He'd gotten even less information from the shelter's director than Melanie had gotten from whoever had called her, but for whatever reason—and he had no real answer—he just wasn't going to allow his mind to go there. And he wasn't going to allow her mind to go there, either—not unless it was absolutely unavoidable.

"We're not going to make any conclusions until all the information is in," he told her. "Anything less than that and you're not going to be any good to anyone— least of all yourself. Now, if the ambulance hasn't gotten there, I'm going to need you to help, not to fall apart. Do you understand?" he asked, his voice sharp. It was almost a demand.

"I understand," she answered, trying her very best

not to allow any horrific extraneous thoughts to enter her mind.

She needed to steel herself off for whatever lay ahead.

They got back to the shelter in record time. Mitch ran two lights, something he had never done before in his entire life, not even when he was young. But an urgency had seized him and he couldn't shake the feeling that every single moment counted.

Feeling like a spinning top, he tried to look everywhere at once. The last thing he needed was to be involved in a collision himself.

His heart pounding, he came to a screeching halt in the same parking lot he'd left just a little while earlier. Pausing only to grab his medical bag from the backseat, he ran into the shelter. Melanie was right beside him.

Out of the corner of his eye, Mitch noted that the ambulance he had expected to already be here hadn't arrived yet. Where the hell was it?

Haunted faces clustered around him as he and Melanie raced into the building.

"Where are they?" he demanded.

One of the residents who worked at the shelter as a janitor pointed to the rear of the building. "Out back," he cried. "They're still in the street."

A confluence of voices, all speaking over one another, tried to tell him what was happening. For now, he tuned them all out.

"Blankets!" Melanie cried, yelling the order to no one in particular. "Bring out blankets!" It was all she could think to do. There was a chill in the air and the family needed to be kept warm.

She'd only felt this utterly helpless once before in her life and she fought against the feeling, afraid that it would overwhelm her.

She ran out in front of Mitch, fearful of what she was going to see, just as fearful of hanging back and not getting there in time.

The three bodies looked mangled and broken as they lay on the cracked asphalt, frozen in a grotesque, bloody dance.

Scanning the trio, Mitch tried to decide where he would do the most good. None of them appeared to be breathing.

"Where the hell is the ambulance?" Mitch demanded angrily, straining to hear the sounds of a siren.

There were none.

Dropping to his knees beside the closest body, he quickly assessed April's brother, Jimmy, then Brenda, her mother, and finally, with an increasingly heavier heart, April herself.

The expression on his face grew grimmer with each passing moment.

Melanie felt as if her heart was strangling.

"Mitch?" she cried, distraught and silently begging him for some sort of reassurance.

But he just shook his head. "The mother's gone," he told her.

Checking over the little boy again, he looked up, frustrated beyond words. This wasn't right, this wasn't right, he couldn't help thinking. He felt as if someone had just hollowed out his insides with a dull knife. He thought he was immune to this, that he'd managed to distance himself from feeling anything when he lost a patient, but damn these people and damn Melanie, they had cut through the insulating wall he'd built up around himself.

Grief threatened to undo him.

"I can't get a heartbeat," he told Melanie, each word felt as if he was carving it letter by letter into his own flesh. He began giving the little girl CPR, but it was no use. He wasn't getting a response.

Melanie dropped to her knees beside the little girl, tears flowing fast and furiously, almost blinding her. "April?"

It wasn't a question, it was a plea.

He shook his head. "I'm not getting anything," he told her, feeling sick to his stomach.

All around them, other residents had come out of the shelter and gathered to watch the doctor unsuccessfully try to bring back these three people.

Melanie heard the ambulance siren in the distance. The sound almost echoed in her head.

It all felt surreal.

The next moment, anger exploded in her chest. She wasn't going to accept it! She wasn't going to accept Mitch's pronouncement!

She'd had to accept the death sentence the chaplain had given her over ten months ago, but she absolutely refused to accept this. She didn't care if Mitch was a doctor, she wasn't going accept what he'd just told her.

It wasn't true!

"No! April, c'mon, baby, fight this." Clutching the child to her, she lowered her face to the little girl's ear. "You have to fight this for your mama and for

Jimmy. You have to live for them, do you hear me?"
Melanie sobbed. "You have to live!"

"Melanie," Mitch began, attempting to get her to
release April's inert body and draw her away from the
child. It broke his heart twice over to watch Melanie's
grief. "She's gone."

"No, she's not!" Melanie cried fiercely, anger flash-
ing in her eyes. "She's not! I'm not going to let her go,
do you hear me? I'm not!" Melanie cried passionately.
Turning toward April, she told her, "I'm not letting
you go! You come back to me, you hear?"

Mitch gently but firmly drew Melanie to her feet,
wanting to put distance between her and the deceased
family. At a complete loss how to help her bear up to
this tragedy, he looked to Theresa for help.

"I'm so sorry, Melanie," Theresa began compassion-
ately as she tried to put her arms around the younger
woman. "You need to let go now, dear. You need to—"

"Mama?"

Melanie swung around. She could just barely make
out the weak little voice, the sound wedged between
the tears and protestations of sorrow that were echoing around the horrifying scene.

"Mama," April whimpered, "I hurt. I hurt."

Barely audible sobs mixed in with the tiny voice.
Tears of pain were rolling down the small, dirty cheeks.
April's eyes were shut, but a part of her was definitely
alive, definitely present if not fully conscious.

"Mitch!" Melanie all but shrieked.

Stunned, Mitch fell back to his knees, quickly
checking April's vital signs as the sound of the approaching siren grew louder and louder.

"She's alive," Mitch cried in disbelief.

He looked up at Melanie, unable to explain what had just happened. A minute ago, there had been no heartbeat, no sound of breathing, no signs of life whatsoever.

And now, April was definitely back among the living.

She was trying to say something, her small heart fluttering wildly like the wings of a hovering hummingbird.

He'd been a doctor for several years now and in all that time he had never witnessed a miracle before. As a general rule, he didn't believe in them.

And yet, he had no other name for it. How else could he explain that one moment, the little girl was gone, the next she was alive again?

Back up on his feet, he took Melanie's hand and drew her to him. He moved out of the way as the ambulance attendants entered, pushing a gurney before them. The EMS who was apparently in charge, Eric, according to the name stitched on his badge, looked at Mitch. It was apparent by his expression that he and his team had only been notified of one victim, not three.

"I'll send for two more ambulances," the EMS told Mitch.

"No need," Mitch informed him grimly. "There's only one survivor." He nodded toward April. "The little girl's alive, the other two are gone."

The driver stepped aside for a moment and grabbed his dispatch radio placing another necessary call.

As quickly and succinctly as possible, Mitch told the head EMS attendant what had happened and gave him all the vital signs he'd noted.

Eric nodded. "Okay, we'll take her to County General."

"No," Mitch said, cutting in. He had no operating privileges at County General and he intended to be in the operating salon with April. "Take her to Bedford Memorial. It's closer."

"I know it's closer," Eric acknowledged. "But Doc, we're contracted with County. We're supposed to take accident victims to County General, especially if they're from the shelter."

The other attendant, who doubled as the driver, nodded, as if to back up what Eric had just said.

Mitch took out his wallet, extracted one of his business cards and handed it over to the head EMS attendant.

"I don't have time to argue and neither does she. I'm associated with Bedford Memorial and she's my patient. Take her there," he ordered. "If anyone gives you any trouble, refer them to me," he said.

The attendant looked down at the card, then slipped it into the breast pocket of his uniform. "You got it, Doc."

Mitch exchanged glances with Melanie as the attendants gently lifted April, transferring her from the ground onto the gurney. As they secured her small body, the little girl was sobbing in pain, calling for her mother.

"Are you up to driving?" Mitch asked, still regarding Melanie.

She was having trouble getting her emotions under control. This had been a wild roller-coaster ride and it wasn't over yet.

"Yes," she managed to get out. "Why?"

"I'm going with April," he began. He wanted Melanie to follow the ambulance either in his vehicle or her own.

Melanie was right beside the gurney as the attendants snapped the legs into position, raising the gurney off the ground.

"I want to come in the ambulance, too," she protested. "April needs me," she added.

The attendant settled the problem for them. "Not enough room for all of you. It's going to be a tight squeeze with the doc here."

She knew Mitch's presence beside April was far more necessary than her own. Still, she felt numb and beside herself as she nodded.

"All right," she agreed. "I'll follow you to the hospital with your car."

Theresa put her hand on Melanie's shoulder. "I'll be right behind you," she promised. It was clear that she didn't want Melanie to be alone in the waiting area.

The sound of approaching sirens was heard again. Disoriented, Melanie looked at the director. But it was Mitch who answered her unspoken question.

"That would be the medical examiner," he told her grimly, having noted the driver making a call earlier.

Just then, April, who had faded on them, regained consciousness. Her eyes fluttered open this time.

"Mama?" she cried, looking at Mitch. It was obvious that she was unable to focus.

Mitch didn't want to tell the little girl what had happened, didn't want to risk what that might do to her fragile condition if she knew that both her mother and her brother were dead.

Instead, he lightly touched April's hand, leaned over the child and told her, "April, it's Dr. Mitch. We're taking you to the hospital. We're going to make you all better."

"Okay," she said, her voice so weak that he had to lean in closer, directly over her lips in order to hear her.

"Doc," the driver politely prodded him, "we've got to get going."

"My thoughts exactly," Mitch said, nodding.

He walked directly behind the gurney as the two EMS attendants steered it over toward the ambulance. Mitch stepped back as the two attendants loaded April's gurney onto the back.

The moment the gurney was secured within the ambulance, Mitch quickly climbed in after it.

"Mama?" she whispered, the forlorn note ripping into his heart.

He wrapped his fingers around April's small hand. "Hold on to my hand, April. Everything's going to be all right."

"Okay," she whispered in a trusting voice that threatened to bring tears to his eyes.

He looked up and his eyes met Melanie's just as the attendant closed the doors.

Within ten seconds, the ambulance was leaving the parking lot.

And the medical examiner's black van was pulling in.

Chapter Twelve

Waiting was utter hell.

Every second that dragged by was etched in pure agony.

The longer the operation took, the more Melanie felt as if she was going to leap out of her skin. She needed to have someone come out of the operating room—and soon—to give her an update.

True to her word, Theresa had remained with her, doing what she could to attempt to distract her, at least to some degree.

But mainly what the older woman was trying to do was build upon the sliver of hope Melanie had been clinging to.

The surgical waiting area was fairly empty this late in the evening. Only those whose relatives or friends had been brought in through the emergency room to undergo unscheduled surgery due to some sort of accident—one woman had brought in her sister with a ruptured appendix, another man had run into his family room from the patio only to discover that the plate glass sliding door was *not* open—were in the room, sitting on less than comfortable orange upholstered plastic chairs.

Everyone was waiting for some news coming from the operating rooms.

Tension was thick within the waiting area, but Melanie hardly took notice of the other people, and while Theresa politely engaged with them in the sparse conversation when it was aimed in their direction, Melanie couldn't gather her thoughts together enough to carry on any semblance of dialogue.

"What's taking them so long?" she asked Theresa, finally putting her agitation into words. "Shouldn't they be finished operating on April by now?"

"You want fast, or do you want good, dear?" Theresa asked her sympathetically.

Melanie sighed. Theresa was right. Some things couldn't be rushed. But that didn't mean she had to be happy about it.

"Good," she answered, never taking her eyes off the swinging double doors. "I want good." Three hours ago, April had been wheeled through those doors with Mitch and two nurses in attendance.

That was the last time that she'd heard anything.

When Theresa rose to her feet, she looked at the older woman quizzically. "Are you going home?"

The infinitesimal part of her that wasn't preoccupied with what was happening behind the operating salon's doors felt a twinge of guilt at having the other woman stay with her in the hospital like this.

After all, Theresa did have a family and a life to get back to. She didn't.

"No, I'm just going to see if I can find out any information about April." With that, Theresa went to the ER admission clerk's desk.

The desk was located too far away for Melanie to catch any of the exchange between the two women. Melanie found herself holding her breath until Theresa walked back to her.

Taking the seat next to Melanie again, she told her, "They're still operating on April."

"Why's it taking so long?" Melanie asked. April was small for her age. The doctors in the operating room had had enough time to rebuild her from scratch, Melanie thought irrationally.

Why wasn't Mitch coming out to tell her that everything was all right?

Maybe he can't, the voice in her head taunted her. Fear gripped her heart.

"There was more internal damage than they initially thought," Theresa explained. She patted Melanie's hand. "But April's still hanging in there. You do the same, dear," she told Melanie, putting her arm around the younger woman's shoulders.

It was another two hours before Mitch finally came out of the operating room and into the waiting area. Melanie instantly shot up to her feet, eager and afraid at the same time.

Mitch looked exhausted and drained as he untied the upper portion of his surgical mask. It hung limply around his neck like a symbol of the fight he'd just fought.

"She's in recovery," he told Melanie and Theresa. The latter took hold of Melanie's hand, as if to infuse her with strength as they listened to Mitch's update. "Her condition is critical, but stable."

The words seemed to just bounce off her head, without penetrating.

"What does that mean?" Melanie cried.

"That means she's hanging in there and with any luck, she'll be upgraded to serious but stable." He offered Melanie a weak smile. "Why don't you have Mrs. Manetti take you home, Melanie? There's nothing you can do here tonight."

He was wrong there. "I can keep vigil," Melanie told him stubbornly. "When April wakes up, she's going to need to see a familiar face."

"I'll be by to look in on her," Mitch assured her. One of the ER doctors had called in sick so, since he was already here, he had volunteered to take the shift. Melanie looked as if she'd been to hell and back and he wanted her to get her rest before she collapsed out here.

"But you can't stay in her room with her. I can," she told him.

He looked at Theresa. "Can you please talk some sense into her?" he requested.

To his surprise, Theresa didn't side with him. "Sorry, Doctor, but she's making perfect sense to me. If I were in her place, I'd be doing the same thing." Turning toward Melanie, she said, "I can stay a little longer with you if you like."

"No, that's okay, really. You've done more than enough," Melanie assured her. "Please go home."

Turning toward Mitch, she asked, "Do they have a room assigned to April yet?"

"You'll have to check with the admission's clerk for that," he told her. And then he paused just before going back to the locker room. "I still think you should go home, too. April's not going to regain consciousness until at least sometime tomorrow."

"That's okay. You thought she was dead and she wasn't. Maybe she'll come around sooner than you think as well." She pressed her lips together, doing her best to keep tears of relief from falling. "Anything's possible."

"Yeah," he said, looking over his shoulder toward the operating room. It had been an uphill battle in there, but he'd won. For now. "Anything is."

"Here."

The deep male voice penetrated the misty layer that had settled in and encompassed Melanie's brain.

It took Melanie a couple of seconds to realize that as uncomfortable as it was—and it felt as if she was sitting in a gravel pit on top of unrefined rocks—she had somehow managed to fall asleep in the chair in Melanie's room.

Hours earlier she had followed the orderlies bringing April and her hospital bed up in the service elevator after the little girl had finally been released from the recovery area. She couldn't remember exactly what time that was, only that the moon was still up.

The sun was lighting up the hospital room now.

From then until now, she'd sat in the chair, just watching April. As in every room, there was a television set mounted on the wall opposite April's bed.

But Melanie just couldn't get herself to turn it on. Her mind felt too scattered to pay any attention to some episodic adventure unfolding within the confines of forty-two minutes, sans commercials.

Melanie didn't want any distractions getting in her way. She wanted her full focus to be on April so that when the little girl came to, she would be aware of it, not just notice it as an afterthought during a mindless commercial.

She had no idea when she had fallen asleep. All she knew was that her body hated her for it now because every single part of it felt stiff and achy, as if she'd just gone through a mammoth marathon involving all the sports meant to make her sweat.

Blinking, Melanie focused on the owner of the voice and what "here" referred to.

Belatedly, she realized that it was Mitch and he was holding out a paper cup with coffee in it.

"I figured you might need this right about now," he told her, still holding the cup in front of her. "You take lots of cream in your coffee, don't you?" he asked her.

She took the cup from him and just held it for a second, allowing the subdued heat to penetrate her palms. The warmth spread out to her limbs from there.

Mitch was wearing the same thing he'd worn earlier, before he'd changed into his scrubs. Hadn't he gone home, either?

"How did you know?" she asked, nodding at the container of coffee.

In her experience, most men, when they got coffee for a woman they weren't involved with, usually got her the same kind of coffee they drank. Mitch's coffee was as black as an abyss. Hers was a caramel cream color.

"Just a hunch." He looked over toward April. "I take it she hasn't woken up yet."

"No, she hasn't." She looked at him with a new measure of respect for his abilities. "Can you tell that just by looking at her?"

"No," he corrected, "I can tell that because there are no reports of a wild-eyed blonde running into the hallway, yelling for a doctor."

She took a sip, letting the coffee wind its way through her system. Somewhat fortified, she felt able to confront him with another question. "Is that what I am, a wild-eyed blonde?"

He thought of taking the description he'd used back, or paving over it somehow, but he had a feeling she valued honesty. So he was honest.

"Well, for a while there at the crosswalk, that was a pretty apt description of you." He checked the monitors that were attached to the tiny body, gathering all of April's basic vital statistics and measuring against the last ones. He added something to her IV solution before turning back to Melanie. "I told you she was going to sleep through the night," he reminded her.

Melanie shrugged. "I just wanted to be here for her in case she woke up. The last thing she saw was her mother and brother being hit by that vehicle. That had to be pretty scary for a five-year-old."

"Not too great for an adult, either," he commented. For just the briefest second, there was a chink in his armor.

Melanie raised her eyes to his, curious. "Is that from experience?" she asked.

He thought of just shrugging off her question, saying that he was just talking in general, but maybe saying so, denying it ever happened would have been disrespectful of the one close friend he'd had.

"Yeah."

Now he had really aroused her curiosity. "Want to talk about it?"

"No." His voice was flat, allowing no room for persuasion.

"Okay."

Her response, given so readily, surprised Mitch. It seemed somehow out of character for Melanie. "Just like that?"

"You deserve your privacy. Everyone does," she told him. "When you're ready to talk about it—*if* you're ready to talk about it—you will. And if you want me to be the one you talk to, I'm not that hard to find."

He paused for a moment, making notations into April's chart. The notations in turn would be transcribed to the hospital's software system by April's nurse, but he didn't have time to do the necessary typing right now. He hadn't really ever gotten comfortable with the system.

When he returned the chart to the metal hook at the foot of the bed, he just began to talk. "He was my best friend in medical school—my *only* friend in medical school," he underscored. "It was winter break and we had a couple of drinks at the local pub before splitting up and going our separate ways. He was heading back home to Iowa until after the first of the year. He never even made it to his car."

"What happened?" she asked in a hushed voice,

watching his face closely so as not to overstep. She was acutely aware of how sensitive feelings in this case could be.

"A drunk driver peeling out of the parking lot hit him. Apparently never even knew it, or so he claimed when the police caught up with him. My friend—Jake, Jake Garner," he said, realizing that he had omitted Jake's name from the narrative, "died on the way to the hospital," he concluded quietly.

Her eyes filled with tears for the friend he had lost. "Mitch, I'm so sorry," she told him, her voice scarcely above a whisper. Without realizing it, she'd put her hand on his forearm in a gesture of shared sympathy.

"Yeah, me, too." He shrugged, as if to push the memory of that night back. "It was a long time ago."

"But not long enough to stop hurting," she pointed out. "It never is." Taking a breath, she changed the subject—for both their sakes. "Have they found the driver who did this to April and her family?"

He shook his head. "Not as far as I know," he answered. "Sometimes, these people get away with it."

Melanie felt anger building up inside of her. "It doesn't seem fair."

"No, it doesn't," he agreed. And then he looked at her. She seemed tired. As tired as he felt. "So, can I talk you into going home now?" he asked.

Melanie shook her head, her mouth curving slightly. "April hasn't woken up yet."

"She might not wake up for days," Mitch pointed out patiently.

Chances were that she would, but he was also aware that there were statistics about trauma patients slipping into comas that lasted for months, sometimes even for years. And then there were the ones who never woke up. He refrained from mentioning them, or even thinking about them himself.

"You have a cafeteria here, I'll find someone to bring me something," she told him.

He shook his head as an exasperated sigh escaped his lips. "You have got to be the most stubborn woman I have ever met."

To which she responded, "Some people think that's my greatest asset."

"Some people like Brussels sprouts, but I don't," he informed her pointedly.

Feeling better just talking to him, Melanie played along.

"Really? Because I have a great recipe for Brussels sprouts," she told him. When he grimaced, she went on to describe it. "It involves bread crumbs and melted margarine. You take the Brussels sprouts—"

"I don't like Brussels sprouts."

Both Mitch and Melanie swung around to look at the small occupant in the hospital bed a few feet away. April's eyes were still closed, but she had made a face, the kind children made when confronted with a vegetable they just can't abide, no matter how healthy it was supposed to be for them.

Melanie instantly gravitated to the side of April's bed. "Did you say something, April?" she asked, barely containing her excitement.

There was no response to her question.

"You heard her, right?" she asked Mitch, looking at him. "I wasn't just imagining that, was I?"

Before he could reassure her that he had heard

April weakly proclaim her dislike of Brussels sprouts, April spoke again.

Each word was a struggle for her. "Mama says... I don't...hafta...eat them if... I don't...wanna."

Melanie took the little girl's hand, holding on to it tightly as if anything less might cause April to break away and slip back into unconsciousness.

"April, honey, open your eyes. Open your eyes and look at me," Melanie pleaded. "Please, baby."

Disoriented, the little girl struggled to raise her eyelids.

As he watched her, it was obvious to Mitch that April had lapsed into that sleep-awake state where she was having a great deal of difficulty opening her eyes because they each felt as if they weighed a ton.

"Open your eyes, April," he said, coaxing her as he buffered her other side. "You can do it. I know that they feel heavy but you can open them if you really try hard enough."

For her part, Melanie squeezed the little girl's hand, as if silently adding her voice to Mitch's. She didn't want to confuse April with too many voices coming at her at once, but it was very hard for her to keep quiet.

And then, finally, the small eyelids opened and April looked around. Seeing Melanie and the doctor, she smiled weakly at them.

The next moment, she asked Melanie the question the latter had been dreading.

"Where's Mama?"

Chapter Thirteen

This was why she'd insisted on staying in April's room, keeping vigil over her. Specifically to field this very question.

Now that it was here, Melanie felt her stomach tightening in a hard, unmanageable knot. She was at a loss as to how to answer April, how to put what was undoubtedly the most horrible news the little girl would ever hear into words.

How did she go about telling a five-year-old that her mother was gone, that she was never coming back because she had died?

The inside of Melanie's mouth had gone bone-dry, but she knew she had to tell April, had to find a way to tell her the truth, but to soften it in some way. Right now, she was all that April had.

Melanie lightly skimmed her fingers along the little girl's forehead. "Did your mama ever tell you about heaven, April?"

April tried to nod, but the motion seemed to hurt too much.

"Yes," she whispered. Her cadence was slow and labored. A sadness seeped into her voice as she continued, as if she somehow sensed what was waiting for her at the end of the conversation. "She said it was a pretty place. That's where Daddy is. Heaven."

Tears gathered in Melanie's eyes as she broke the news. "Well honey, your mama and Jimmy went to be with your daddy." It was getting really difficult to talk. The very words felt unwieldy, as if they were getting stuck in her throat.

A tear slid down April's cheek. "Without me?"

Oh Lord, Melanie thought, April sounded so lost, so crushed.

"It wasn't your time to go yet, honey." That sounded so terrible and so stilted. She raised her eyes helplessly to Mitch. What had made her think that she'd be any good at this?

Before Mitch could find anything reassuring to say, April asked in a small, lost voice, "What's going to happen to me?"

"We're going to take care of you, honey. Make sure you get all better," Melanie promised her. "Dr. Mitch saved your life."

"Why couldn't he save Mama's?" April cried.

"Because she had already gone to heaven before he got there," Melanie said, sparing Mitch from having to answer the little girl.

Rather than say anything, Mitch took the little girl's hand in his and squeezed it, silently conveying a great many things that couldn't be put into words. Telling her that she was safe.

"And when Dr. Mitch says you can go home," Melanie told her, "you can come home with me."

Mitch glanced at her sharply, but Melanie focused her attention on the frightened, battered little girl in the hospital bed. She was trying her best to reassure her and give her a feeling of being safe.

"Okay," April whispered. The next moment, her green eyes had shut and she'd fallen asleep.

Mitch frowned. "And just how are you going to manage to pull *that* off?" he asked.

Melanie shrugged, moving away from the bed. "I'll find a way."

He stared at her in disbelief. "You're serious." It was more of a stunned statement than a question.

Melanie never wavered. "Very."

Taking her by the arm, he drew her aside, not wanting anything he had to say to possibly be overheard by the little girl. Mitch shook his head.

"You can't just walk off with a kid anytime you feel like it," he pointed out.

"I'm not planning on 'walking off with her,'" Melanie protested heatedly. "I'm going to apply to be her foster mother. And then, when the time's right, I'm going to adopt her."

For a moment, he was at a loss for words. He had no idea where to begin to take apart this fantasy Melanie had constructed in her head.

"You're letting your emotions run away with you," he accused.

She wasn't about to argue that part with him. "Maybe. But the more I think about it, the more it just feels right." She could see he totally disagreed with her. She didn't need his permission, but getting his backing would help her. "Look, the social services system is overloaded right now and April is going to need to be taken care of until she makes a full recovery."

Melanie could get him exasperated faster than anyone he'd ever dealt with. "Yes, I know that, but that still doesn't change the fact that—"

She cut him off, needing to get him on her side. "If no one notifies Social Services, they won't know about her situation. Let me take care of her for a while," she implored him. "One step at a time, Mitch. First, she needs to get well."

Mitch dragged a hand through his hair. What she was proposing was insane, even though he knew why she was doing it.

"This is crazy, you know that, don't you?"

"It can be done," she insisted.

"All right, just how do you intend to provide for her?" he asked. April moaned. Afraid that his voice might be waking her up, he lowered it. "You're at the shelter everyday."

She'd already worked that out while sitting here, waiting for April to regain consciousness. "I can get my old job back. The principal at the school left the door open for me, told me I could come back anytime I wanted to. April gives me a reason to come back." She caught hold of his wrist, as if to anchor him in place until she could convince him to see things her way. "Please, Mitch. This little girl just lost everything. She and I have made a connection. Let me help her."

She was relentless, he'd give her that, Mitch thought with a weary sigh. Still, he gave talking her out of it one more try.

"Melanie, you've got a good heart," he began, "nobody's disputing that. But there are rules we're supposed to follow."

Melanie pressed her lips together, debating telling him something—and making him an accessory after the fact. After a moment, she decided to risk it, praying that he wouldn't give her away and that he would take her side.

"While I was sitting here, one of the hospital administrators came in with some paperwork for April that needed to be filled out. I put myself down as her next of kin."

He stared at her, stunned. "You did what?"

"I said I was her late mother's cousin." It was a vague enough connection, she thought. "All you have to do is not saying anything."

"So what you're telling me now isn't just a spur of the moment thing," he concluded.

His expression was dark. She had no idea if she'd just made a mistake. Would he give her away? "Like I said, I've had a while to think about it," she told him.

Mitch blew out a ragged breath as he glanced back at April for a moment, then back at Melanie. He could see that there was no talking her out of what she intended to do. If he tried to stand in her way, she'd probably find a way around it.

And, at bottom was the fact that she was right. Once in the system, April would be lost in it. He'd heard enough secondhand horror stories about the way children were treated to know he didn't want that happening to anyone, least of all a little girl whose crayon drawing resided on his refrigerator.

Looking at Melanie, he shook his head. "Like I said, you are the stubbornest woman I've ever met."

And then he looked back at April. "Looks like the sedative I gave her earlier has kicked in."

"You gave her a sedative?" Melanie questioned.

He nodded. "When I first came in. She needs to sleep in order to heal. I'm surprised she woke up just now. Looks like you and she are cut out of the same cloth," he commented. "She's going to be asleep until at least the morning. I'm going home," he told Melanie. "Why don't I drop you off at your place? No offense, but you look like hell."

She laughed softly. "You do know how to flatter a girl."

"Yes, I do," he said. "But this isn't one of those times. Now, if you want me to back up your story, you're going to have to do as I say."

Her eyes narrowed as she looked at him uncertainly. "Are you blackmailing me?"

Mitch never hesitated in his response. "As a matter of fact, yes I am."

For a moment, he didn't know whether or not to expect an argument from her. And then he saw her smile. "Then I guess I don't have a choice."

"No, you don't," he agreed.

Melanie hesitated as she paused for a moment longer to look at April. "I don't want her waking up and finding herself alone."

That was no problem. "I can have a nurse posted here with her. Anything else?"

She shook her head, suddenly incredibly weary.

Yesterday's events were finally catching up to her. "No, you seem to have covered all the bases."

"Good. Then let's go."

Mitch stopped at the nurse's station long enough to request that a nurse remain with April, saying he was worried that her fever might spike. If it did, he left instructions to be called immediately, regardless of the time.

That done, he took Melanie's arm and directed her toward the elevator. Pressing the down button, he asked in a low voice, "Satisfied?"

"Satisfied," she replied.

"I'm not biting off more than I can chew, you know," Melanie said in her own defense, breaking the silence in the car fifteen minutes after they had left the hospital parking lot.

They were almost at her door. She had debated saying nothing and just thanking him for the ride once he pulled up at the curb, but since Mitch *was* going along with her request to, in effect, become April's guardian, she felt as if she did owe him some sort of assurance about what she was doing.

Lost in his own thoughts about April and the woman he was, by virtue of his silence, agreeing to lie for, he didn't hear what Melanie had just said.

"What?"

"I know that's what you're thinking," she told him. "That I'm biting off more than I can chew, but I'm not," she said emphatically. "I've always wanted to have children."

"There is a more traditional route to that end, you know," he pointed out.

She knew he meant getting married. "I wanted to, but it didn't work out," she said, her tone indicating that she wanted to leave it at that.

He knew Melanie was referring to her late fiancé and out of deference to her, he didn't pursue the matter. It was none of his business anyway, he reminded himself. If she wanted to take on the responsibility of taking care of the little girl, maybe it was for the best for both of them. He'd done his part. He'd put April back together. Melanie could supply the love that was needed.

But as he pulled up at the curb before Melanie's house, he saw that she was trembling.

Turning off the engine, he shifted to look at her. "Are you all right?"

"It's just been a hard eighteen hours," she replied. "And I'm tired." The last thing she wanted was for him to think she was falling apart. It was bad enough that she felt as if she was. She'd get this under control, she promised herself. To her surprise, Mitch got out of the car, came around to her side and opened her door. She looked down at the hand he held out for her. "I can get out on my own power."

"Maybe," he allowed. "But I'm still walking you to your house."

This whole thing with April being at the brink of death and then being revived had brought back memories. Memories that made her feel vulnerable. She didn't think that having him walk her to her home was a particularly good idea.

She needed to put distance between them now, while she still could.

"You don't have to. Really. I'll be all right."

He leaned into the vehicle, his hand still out. "Humor me."

She could see that he wasn't about to be talked out of it. All she needed to do was keep it together a little while longer, Melanie told herself, and then she'd be home free.

Resigned, Melanie got out of his car and then walked ahead of him to her front door. Turning around to face him, she gestured at it.

"Well, here it is, the door."

"Unlock it," he told her.

He was really making this hard for her. "You said you want to walk me to my door and you did. Chivalrous obligation met."

"No, I said that I was walking you to your house. That means I want you to open the door and go inside," he told her sternly. "I don't want to hear a story on the local morning news about the heart-of-gold volunteer who passed out in front of her front door."

"What are you talking about?" she demanded.

He pointed out the obvious. "You're still trembling."

Melanie shrugged indifferently. "I'm cold," she lied.

Mitch frowned. He wasn't buying her excuse. "Then you're coming down with something because it's really pretty warm tonight."

This wasn't getting her anywhere and she could feel herself weakening. Could feel herself growing more and more in need of the feel of strong arms around her, holding back the darkness.

"Fine, I'll unlock the door." Inserting the key into the lock, she turned it, then opened the door.

Turning around in her front foyer, Melanie started to ask him if he was satisfied. But the words never materialized. Instead, just as she was afraid of, the full impact of the past few emotional hours hit her.

The thought of what could have been April's fate if they hadn't arrived at the accident when they did and if Mitch hadn't been the skilled surgeon that he was hit her full force and she began to cry.

As a rule, Mitch avoided being around a woman's tears. They made him uncomfortable and he had no idea how to even begin to offer any sort of words of comfort or condolences.

But the past several hours had definitely left their mark on him. He had fought death and won—and he wouldn't have if not for Melanie and her refusal to give up.

Moreover, because of Melanie and her almost militant cheerfulness, the past several weeks had left an impression on him, as well. She'd softened him, filing down his hard edges. So rather than mumble some inane words of comfort that he neither felt nor believed, or offer Melanie the handkerchief he had stuffed into his pocket, Mitch found himself crossing the threshold, closing the door with his elbow and taking her into his arms.

He held her close to him as she cried, moving his hands along her back soothingly.

And somewhere in those first couple of minutes, something came completely loose within him, as well.

"It's going to be all right," he told her. "The worst part is over. She's lost her mother and her brother, but she has you and you'll help her heal. We both will," he added quietly.

Melanie raised her head from his chest, tears staining both her cheeks. Mitch had said the one thing that made her feel less alone. Rather than abating her tears, he'd just made them flow more freely. But now they were tears of relief mingled with joy. "You really think so?"

Why hadn't he realized how beautiful she was before? "I do," he told her softly.

"You're the one who really saved her."

He knew he would have given up when he'd thought April was dead. Melanie was as responsible for April being alive today as he was.

"And you made her realize she's not alone. It's a joint effort," he concluded.

"You really believe that?" she asked in a whisper.

"I do."

And then, because he couldn't seem to help himself, he lowered his head and kissed her.

He only meant to brush his lips against hers, to comfort Melanie more than anything else—or so he told himself. But kissing her reminded him just how attracted he really was to her.

He realized now that all along, he'd tried to bury it, to deny it and to talk himself out of it every time he felt things stirring within him—like when he'd kissed her in the exam room.

And all the while, he'd tried to keep her at arm's length. But the tragedy that had befallen April's family and then the battle to save her life had unleashed all his tightly wound emotions. He'd forgotten what it was like to actually *feel* something, what it was like to immerse himself in another person and to allow his emotions to flower.

So, for just a moment, he went with the moment, telling himself he was in complete control—until he realized that he wasn't. Because if he had been in complete control, he could have stopped himself, walked away from what was happening with a few well-placed words and made his way back to his car.

And driven away like the very devil was after him.

But any plans for a quick getaway evaporated in the heat of his desire. The more he kissed Melanie, the more he *needed* to kiss her until the matter was entirely out of his system. He found himself caught up in a sea he couldn't begin to navigate.

It all came racing back to her.

She'd forgotten what it was like. Forgotten what it felt like to be a woman with a woman's needs. Forgotten how it felt to be wanted.

His kiss had brought it all back to her.

She had no illusions. This wasn't something with "forever" attached to it. This was a onetime deal because he had saved April's life and she just desperately needed to make human contact again. To shed all her concerns, her fears and all the dark, shadowy things that haunted her days and her nights, consciously or otherwise.

Just for tonight, she wanted to make love and to be made love to. Tomorrow she would go back to her austere world, knowing there was nothing else waiting for her. Not in this venue, not ever.

But that didn't matter because tomorrow there would be a little girl waiting who needed her. Someone to whom she mattered. Someone who depended on her—and that was more than enough.

But tonight, well tonight she needed something else, something more.

She needed to revisit the ability to have fiery passions explode within her, to just be a woman alone with a man.

So when Mitch's lips touched hers, at first softly, then with more heat, more passion, she kissed him back. And then she kissed him again and again, each kiss more demanding than the last, until she lost all track of just who was seducing whom.

All she knew was that for the duration of the evening, it felt wonderful and she was grateful to Mitch for everything.

For being able to feel normal and real again.

Inhibitions and clothing came off and with each layer, something wondrous took a firmer hold. She shuddered with pleasure as he ran his hands along her body, and she kissed him with passion as a frenzy seemed to take hold of her.

Maybe she'd known all along that this was waiting for her. Maybe that was why she'd backtracked on several occasions, afraid of getting closer to him, afraid of where it might lead because there was always a price to pay for feeling like this and she didn't want to ever be in that position again.

But even so, she couldn't deny what her body already knew. That she was very attracted to this man, not just physically, but emotionally, as well. She saw that he tried to keep a distance between himself and everyone he ministered to—and yet he had gotten involved nonetheless. He had stepped out of his comfort zone for her, for April and for the people at the shelter.

That was a kindness she found even sexier than his handsome face and athletic body. He was a package deal and for the evening, he was hers and she was his.

Chapter Fourteen

It seemed clichéd and almost absurd to Mitch. He knew he would have been skeptical if someone had been relaying all this to him as something *they* were going through.

But he had never felt this way before.

Moreover, he had never believed it was *possible* to feel like this, like something inside of him had suddenly lit up and was close to, Lord help him, singing.

Certainly he could have sworn that there was *music* humming through his veins.

Music as well as an overwhelming need to not just unite with this woman, but to just *be* with her without anything physical happening at all.

He had never felt that way before, never thought that people, that *he,* could feel like this before. But rays of light and something akin to sunshine seemed to be shining all through him. Whatever it was—and he was fairly convinced that it was *her*—he didn't want it to stop, to change or go away even though it meant, most likely, saving himself in the end.

Cradling her against him, he kissed Melanie over and over again, finding himself desiring more with each kiss rather than drawing closer to the point of satiating himself.

His excitement heightening each time he kissed not just her lips but every single part of her soft, yielding and heating body. With each pulsating moment, he felt more and more as if he had crossed some sort of a line, going from a place he was vaguely familiar with to a place he hadn't believed existed. A place that seemed to welcome him with both arms.

A place he never wanted to leave ever again.

He knew he had to be going crazy.

He didn't care.

Finally, close to the brink, he moved his primed and more than ready body over hers. His eyes locking with hers, Mitch took the final step and united them.

His entire body pleaded for instant release but he went about it slowly.

Gently.

Bringing the union to an ever faster growing, more intense rhythm.

And as it increased, he could feel her response, could hear her breathing becoming more rapid, more ragged. The very sound of that brought his own excitement to an even higher level.

Joined together in the most intimate of dances two people could undertake, the tempo seemed to increase of its own accord until they reached the peak together—he could tell by the way she grasped onto his shoulders, arched her body into his and moaned his name that she was climaxing at the exact same moment as he was.

Enraptured by the moment, he found to his surprise that he was more taken with her reaction than just his alone. That was different and once he would have thought that there was something wrong, but he had never felt anything so right in his life as this eternal moment he was sharing with her.

And then it was over, fading into the very air around him.

Spiraling downward, he held on to her, shifting his position so that she was resting her face against his chest.

Words still failed him, but words weren't necessary here. Not when the touch of his hand along her hair conveyed the very intensity of what he was experiencing this second with her.

So they lay there, separated from time and the rest of the world for this very short, very precious interlude. And he held her and just absorbed the goodness of the moment and of the woman who was in his arms, lying against his heart.

Melanie had lost track of time.

Raising her head, she looked at Mitch, almost afraid of what she would see.

But there was no smug expression, no look of distance in his eyes the way there had been when she had first met him. There was a look she had never seen before and she was afraid to put a name to it because she knew what she was hoping for. Something that she had already accepted as not possible.

Not from him—and, besides, she had told herself that above all else, she didn't want it. Didn't want it because she didn't trust it. She knew all the pitfalls that were waiting for her if she did truly become involved with a man. The exhilaration of love—my Lord, was she actually even *thinking* in those terms?—had a very dark downside to it.

It was bitter, burning and she wanted no part of it.

And yet, what was the point of life without it?

"Well, that was unplanned," Mitch murmured as he ran his hand along her silky hair in a movement that was not quite possessive and yet definitely not indifferent.

"I didn't mean for that to happen," Melanie said defensively.

At least, she hadn't meant for it to happen in the absolute sense, she thought.

All of this was a result of an incredible moment of weakness on her part and in no way had she *ever* expected him to respond with this amount of intensity.

And she certainly hadn't expected him to have rocked her world the way he had.

She supposed that at best she had hoped for a few minutes of diversion that would in turn help her stop hurting and caring and just respond on a basic, automatic level.

In no way had she expected something of this magnitude to affect her.

"Well, I did." It was as if he had stepped out of his own body and was watching all this at a respectful distance. Supervising events rather than actually being involved in them.

And yet, what else could he possibly call it? He

was involved. He, who almost took *pride* in being removed, was involved.

Mitch raised her chin with the crook of his forefinger until their eyes met. "Are you sorry?" he asked.

His eyes seemed to look straight into her soul. She couldn't lie, not when he was looking at her like that. "No."

"Then stop talking," he told her.

His hand along the white column of her throat, he tilted her head back and captured her mouth with his just for a moment.

Or so he had thought.

But just as before, a moment stretched out into two which multiplied into four. And that just continued at a breathtaking pace as he found himself wanting her all over again, even more than the first time.

Mitch was completely stunned by the event and completely captivated by the woman he had initially taken into his arms a small eternity ago.

The second time turned out to be as wondrous as the first. He knew what to expect and yet was still stunned by what he was feeling.

Once was a complete surprise.

To feel that twice bordered on a miracle as far as he was concerned. And he knew he wasn't feeling this because he was overworked or overwhelmed by the intensity of what had happened with April.

Granted, he was tired, but he was still far from wiped out—which would have been his go-to excuse for feeling like this.

So what, really, was going on here? If he were

being honest with himself, Mitch knew that he was almost leery of finding out.

It was enough that it had happened and that he was lying there, in the dark, with her in his arms.

Just then, his phone went off.

Both of them jackknifed up in bed in unison to the jarring sound.

"April?" Melanie asked, fear lacing itself around her voice.

Guilt instantly raised its head. What kind of a person was she, to seek refuge in a physical coupling, not once but *twice* while that poor child was lying in a hospital bed, very possibly still closer to death than not.

Mitch reached for his cell phone. "I do still have a day job," he reminded her. He glanced down at the caller ID. "And I think it's calling me. Dr. Stewart," he said, his voice formal as he swiped his phone and answered it.

She could feel the distance coming between them as Mitch listened quietly to whoever was on the other end of the line.

Not only did the man have a day job, she silently upbraided herself, but in all likelihood, he probably had a full life, as well. Just because he had never mentioned it to her didn't mean he didn't have one. He hadn't mentioned a great many things to her.

She knew very little about the man. For all she knew, he was involved with someone already.

No. If he were, she'd know. She was certain that she'd know. He would have allowed something to slip, allowed a telltale piece of information about his personal life to surface.

This was a man who had no personal life. She would have sworn to it.

After all, she couldn't be *that* bad a judge of character, could she?

Melanie watched as he terminated the call. "You have to go," she said. It wasn't a question.

"Van versus truck," he recounted simply.

Her stomach churned just thinking about the incident. "Anyone left alive?"

He nodded. "So far, according to the hospital, all four drivers and passengers."

She slid to the edge of the bed, ready to throw her clothes on at a moment's notice and follow. All he had to do was say the word.

"Can I do anything to help?" she asked.

"Not unless you're a nurse," he answered matter-of-factly as he hurried into his clothes.

"I can pray," she replied simply.

Then, out of the corner of his eye, he saw Melanie getting her clothes together, then quickly getting dressed, as well.

"You need clothes to pray?" he asked, mildly curious as to what she was really up to.

"No, but I need clothes to get back into the hospital," she answered, pulling her hair out of the collar of her pullover. "They frown upon naked people unless they happen to be lying on one of their operating tables."

Mitch stopped putting his shoes on for a moment. "I said there's nothing you can do," he reminded her.

"Not for the people you're going to be operating on who were involved in that awful accident, but I can go back to the hospital in case April wakes up earlier than we thought she would."

"I left a nurse with her, remember? And you need your rest," he told her seriously. "Doctor's orders."

Something warm and precious moved within her and she smiled up at him. "You're not my doctor," she told him sweetly, and then added, "Besides, I rested."

Mitch raised a dubious eyebrow. "When?" he asked. "Seems to me that wasn't exactly the most rest-provoking endeavor we were engaged in just a little while ago."

"Maybe not restful," she allowed, slipping the remainder of her clothing on, "but definitely energizing which, on some levels, is even better," she concluded with a satisfied smile.

Ready, Mitch paused for a moment to study her. He was definitely getting to know sides of her that hadn't been evident initially, but this was something that had been there right from the start.

"What was it you said you were before you took your leave of absence?" he asked her.

She might have mentioned it in passing, but she had never been specific about it. "A second-grade teacher. Why?"

"You sure you weren't really a lawyer?" he asked, pretending to scrutinize her closely. "Because you use words like a weapon and you're stubborn, all useful skills for a top-grade lawyer."

"And a teacher," she told him. "You would be surprised how devious some of those innocent-looking second graders can be."

"Maybe not so surprised," he qualified, pausing to give her a fleeting kiss. It was all he could trust himself to do at the moment. Anything even slightly deeper and he'd be sorely tempted to linger with her a little while longer. Time in his chosen profession was always of the essence.

"Okay," she announced as he headed for the door and she fell into step beside him, "if I can get you to swing by the shelter, I can pick up my car." Opening the front door, Mitch looked at her blankly for a moment, not following her. "When this all started, you took me out to dinner from the shelter in your car."

She'd followed the ambulance in his car and had remained at the hospital with April until he'd driven her home in his car. She hadn't seen her own vehicle in all that time.

"As far as I know, my car is still parked there." Melanie saw him glancing at his watch and realized that time, as it had been with April, was of tantamount importance. "Or I can always call a cab to bring me to the shelter."

He waved away her offer. "No, it's just a little out of the way," Mitch told her, doing a quick calculation. "As long as you're ready."

"So completely ready," she declared, grabbing her purse.

"Okay," he responded.

The thing was he really didn't know if he was. Ready for her, that was. She was taking him to a brand-new place, one he liked but one that also made him wary.

It could be a matter of something being too good to be true. And yet, all he could think about was getting back here, back to her. Back to making love with her.

What the hell was going on here?

He didn't know, couldn't explain. All he could do, with luck, was ride the wave.

Getting from the shelter to the hospital proved a little trickier for Melanie than getting from point A to point B. That was strictly because point A came with a large amount of people who had questions for her.

The moment she was spotted in the shelter's parking lot, about to get into her vehicle, she was seen by several of the children who were playing in the designated playground area. The latter consisted of little more than a couple of swings and an old-fashioned sandbox, but the area was well populated and the moment the children saw Melanie, they came running out to shower her with questions. Everyone wanted to know how April was doing.

Their raised voices and the volley of nonstop questions attracted some of the mothers residing at the shelter and soon Melanie found herself answering questions coming from adults instead of children.

She was aware that the director had come to the hospital to look in on April herself—she'd seen the woman in April's room—but as for the other women, though concerned, they were relying on the reports of others to satisfy their questions.

Melanie didn't want to seem rude, so consequently it took her a bit of time before she could get away. The upshot was that it took Melanie far longer to get to the hospital than she was happy about.

Coming into the little girl's room, she found that April was sound asleep. Whether she was still asleep from when she had initially left her or had woken up and then fallen back to sleep, Melanie had no way of knowing—but she intended to find out.

The nurse that Mitch had left in the room was not there, which really concerned her.

Going to the nurse's station on that floor, Melanie was about to ask after the nurse's whereabouts. At that moment, her cell phone vibrated.

Taking it out, she experienced an eerie moment of uneasiness, as if in anticipation of something major. Melanie glanced down to see that the call was coming from within the hospital. Which was odd.

"Hello?" she asked uncertainly.

"Hello, Ms. McAdams?" a rather young female voice asked.

Melanie had no idea why her stomach instantly tightened the way it did. "Yes?"

"This is Jennifer Donnelly," the caller told her, identifying herself. "The nurse involved in this matter said I should give you a call. I'm from Social Services and this is about April O'Neill. You're familiar with that name?"

Melanie could feel her heart all but constricting within her chest. This was what she'd supposedly been waiting for. But rather than having a case of nerves, the way she'd anticipated, she could feel her temper surging in her chest.

"Yes," she replied evenly. "Of course I know April O'Neill—"

"We were informed that her mother was killed two days ago by a hit-and-run driver. With no father in the picture, she automatically becomes our responsibility. However, the nurse insisted that before we begin any paperwork to take custody, I call you. To be honest, I'm not exactly sure why."

Melanie's hand tightened on her cell phone. "Well, that's really very simple, Ms. Donnelly," she heard herself saying. "She told you that because I'm April O'Neill's next of kin."

Good luck in pulling this off, Melanie thought to herself.

Chapter Fifteen

There was a momentary silence on the other end of the cell phone.

Melanie knew she'd hit the woman with something she hadn't been expecting, even though, if the social worker had looked at the hospital forms that she had filled out for April, Donnelly would have realized that April was not the orphan that she was perceived to be.

"Well, that certainly is a reason to call you," Donnelly agreed, the woman's voice sounding a bit too chipper to her for her peace of mind. "When can we get together?"

Melanie would have loved to have had a few hours to get her act together. Certainly she could have used at least that much time to make herself look presentable instead of probably something a self-respecting cat might hesitate to drag in.

But apparently she wasn't about to have that luxury. Melanie had this very uneasy feeling that if she put this so-called meeting off she would wind up regretting it.

"Now is fine."

It was obviously the right answer because it met with Donnelly's approval.

"All right. Now it is," the woman told Melanie. "We can meet in the chapel. I'm told it's empty at the moment. I can be there in ten minutes."

"So can I," Melanie said, her stomach sinking to new depths.

Melanie arrived at the chapel before the other woman. Her nerves barely had time to settle down before Jennifer Donnelly entered the small, welcoming nondenominational chapel.

The social worker looked to be a little older than she was, Melanie observed. She also looked as if she was the epitome of efficiency, to the possible exclusion of actual sympathy. That worried Melanie.

But she wasn't about to walk out of this chapel until she was granted some sort of custody of April no matter how long it took, that much she knew.

Indicating a pew, Donnelly sat down after she took a seat. The cool, dark eyes made no secret that the social worker was sizing her up.

Her voice was distant, reserved when she finally spoke. "I just want you to understand that I am doing this out of a sense of decency since there is no requirement for anyone in the department to notify perfect strangers as to our intentions regarding a child who comes to our attention. As soon as April is back on her feet, Social Services will be taking custody of her since she has no next of kin as far as we can see," Donnelly informed her with finality, underscoring the last six words.

"You can't do that," Melanie cried.

The more agitated Melanie sounded, the more reserved the other woman became. "And why not?"

"Because she and I have built up a rapport since she first got to the shelter." Her mind scrambling, Melanie remembered the form she'd filled out when April was admitted and what she'd told the woman to bring this meeting about. Why was Donnelly "conveniently" forgetting about that? "And like I told you, I'm April's next of kin."

The social worker's small mouth twisted into a sneer. "Oh, really? Well, we have no record of you." It was clear by her tone that she expected there to be some sort of record since in this day and age, there was a great deal of information available in cyberspace to back up a claim one way or another.

Desperate, Melanie was making it up as she went along. "This only came up recently. Her mother—Brenda—and I lost track of one another for a long time. She was my cousin. Her mother, I mean."

"I see." It was obvious by her expression that Donnelly didn't believe any of it.

The way she was tapping a file in her hand, Melanie had a feeling that the woman had already done some extensive research into April's background. Or as extensive as was possible, given the situation, Melanie thought, mentally crossing her fingers.

Was there something in that file about her, as well? That she worked at the shelter and nothing more? Melanie anxiously searched her brain for something to work with. She couldn't allow April to be taken into the system or she would never see the little girl again. She couldn't bear losing April, losing someone else. That just couldn't happen to her twice. She wouldn't let it.

"So, which is it?" Donnelly asked sarcastically. "You've built up this rapport with April or you're her long-lost cousin, twice removed?"

Melanie raised her chin. Chapel or not, she wasn't about to take this quietly. "I don't think I like your tone."

Donnelly's eyes narrowed with contempt. "Doesn't matter what you like, Ms. McAdams. I represent the best interests of the child."

The hell she did. "So, taking her from the only environment she is familiar with and has learned to trust and throwing her in with a bunch of strangers where she'll be frightened is in her best interests?" Melanie demanded heatedly.

Donnelly drew herself up indignantly. "Ms. McAdams, you have no idea how many people out there pose as one thing and are something else entirely. All they want to do is get their hands on an innocent child and, best-case scenario, they want to use that child for a meal ticket in order to get extra money." The woman paused for half a second. "Worst case, well, I don't even want to get into that."

"My point entirely," Melanie stressed. "My first, my *only* concern, is April."

The expression on the social worker's face said she highly doubted that. "Then let the professionals do their job."

At a loss, Melanie tried another approach to attempt to gain custody of the little girl. "So, you have a home waiting for her right now?"

Annoyance furrowed the almost perfect brow. "No, but—"

"Well, I do," Melanie said, cutting in. "A good, clean, loving home."

The look Donnelly gave her could have easily cut a lesser woman dead in her tracks. "I was about to say that not yet, but by the time April is released from the hospital, arrangements will be made."

Yeah, she'd bet. She'd heard enough horror stories from some of the single mothers at the shelter about the battles they had to wage in order to regain custody of their own children. Some of them were still fighting the court.

"No disrespect as to your 'arrangements,'" Melanie told the woman, "but April won't know any of these people you're thinking of placing her with."

Thin shoulders shrugged indifferently. "An unfortunate situation, I admit, but—"

"She knows me," Melanie insisted. "She feels *safe* with me." Melanie continued, praying some of this was sinking into the woman's hard heart. "I stayed in her hospital room from the time they found her in the street until she woke up. Run any background check on me you want," she challenged. "I have a spotless record and I love her."

Donnelly pressed impatient lips together. It was clear she didn't like wasting time this way. Her next words indicated that some checking into her background had already been done, most likely because of what she'd filled in on the hospital forms. The woman came prepared, Melanie thought in despair.

"You have no source of income, Ms. McAdams. How do you intend to help pay for this child—or are you banking on Social Services to take care of that little detail for you?" she asked contemptuously. "For that matter, if we granted you temporary foster-care custody, how would we even *know* that the money intended for April would *go* to April?"

It was obvious from the way she spoke that Donnelly was all too familiar with that aspect of cheating within the system.

The woman was talking down to her. Melanie struggled to hold on to her temper as she tried to clear up the numerous misunderstandings. "Number one, I am on a leave of absence—"

"According to our records," Donnelly said, cutting her off, "you quit."

"Your records don't go deep enough," Melanie countered. "I tried to quit, but my principal wouldn't let me. She talked me into taking a leave of absence instead and told me my job would be waiting for me when I was ready to come back."

"Your quitting only proves how unstable you are," Donnelly pointed out with almost relish. "April needs a stable environment—"

She should have known this wouldn't have been the end of it. The social worker wouldn't be satisfied until she wound up cutting her up into little pieces.

"My fiancé was killed overseas by a suicide bomber four days before he was scheduled to come home to me for our *wedding*. Tell me, Ms. Donnelly, how would *you* have held up under that?" Melanie challenged angrily. "And I didn't just run off, I came to the homeless shelter to volunteer full-time so that I could feel that at least I was being useful to someone."

The woman was momentarily at a loss as to how to answer. Then, taking a breath, to Melanie's surprise Donnelly said in a somewhat kinder tone, "Be that as it may, there is still the matter of your financial situation—"

Melanie cut her off. "Look, I don't want to be April's foster mother and have you people paying me for taking care of her. I want to take her in so I can adopt her," she emphasized. Why couldn't the woman get that through her head?

Donnelly closed her eyes, as if searching for patience. "Yes, because you're this long-lost relative—"

"Because I love her," Melanie stressed, banking down her anger.

"And if we did this extensive background check you said you wanted and found that you're not related to April's mother at all?" Donnelly challenged. The look on her face said what she knew the outcome of that check would be.

Melanie rose to her feet, ready to just walk out before she really lost her temper and exploded.

"Aren't you listening?" Melanie cried. "I want to *adopt* her. Most people who adopt children aren't related to them. Most of the time, they haven't even had time to develop a relationship with the child before they adopt them. April and I have—"

"—bonded, yes, so you said," Donnelly said in a singsong voice. "Still—"

"Is there a problem here?"

Melanie could have sobbed when she heard Mitch's voice coming from behind her. She swung around immediately and had to struggle not to throw her arms around his neck out of pure relief.

Finally someone to back her up.

She had no idea what he could say that she hadn't, but the very fact that he was a surgeon here at the hospital and not just *any* surgeon, but one with a rather well-known reputation, meant that this woman from hell had to listen to him.

Didn't she?

Donnelly rose to her feet instantly. "No problem here, Doctor," the woman said crisply, but with an obvious respect that had been missing from her voice when she spoke to Melanie. "Ms. McAdams here is taking exception to the Department of Social Services taking custody of one of the patients here."

Mitch's somber expression was almost intimidating, Melanie thought and for once, she was extremely glad of that.

"April O'Neill, yes I know," he replied.

Donnelly's dark, probing eyes took complete measure of the man in front of her before she spoke. "Then you are familiar with the little girl?"

"I should be," Mitch informed the woman. "I operated on her. Prior to that, I treated her and Jimmy, her late brother, at the Bedford Rescue Mission."

"I see. Very kind of you—" Donnelly began, about to use the throwaway line as a transition to get to the heart of her subject. It was obvious that she felt flattery was the way to get on his good side.

The social worker had a thing or two to learn about the man, Melanie thought.

"Kindness had nothing to do with it, Ms. Donnelly." The nurse who had alerted him about the social worker meeting with Melanie at the chapel had given him the woman's name. "Especially in the beginning." He glanced at Melanie. "That, I think you should know, was all Ms. McAdams's doing. I'd initially volunteered for what I thought would be a single visit to the shelter. It was Ms. McAdams who came to the hospital, found me and literally *dragged* me back over to the shelter to impress upon me just how necessary it was for a physician to make regular visits there so that the women and children residing at the shelter could receive proper care and proper follow-up care."

At the time Melanie's presumption had irritated the hell out of him, but now that he looked back at it, that had been the beginning of his own transformation.

"We have programs—" the woman began rather indignantly, apparently taking what he was saying as an attack on her department's services.

Unable to hold her tongue any longer, Melanie interjected, "Which their pride keeps them from utilizing."

"Oh, and bringing a doctor to them is different?" Donnelly asked sarcastically, directing the question at her.

"Yes, it is," Melanie retorted. "If he's right there, they can't very well avoid him. And more importantly, Dr. Stewart doesn't make them feel like they're charity cases. That's often the problem when they go to some authorized clinic on the other side of town to see doctors who would rather be somewhere else, getting paid what they felt they were actually worth. It makes them feel as if they're worthless inconveniences instead of normal human beings who just happen to have fallen on hard times—sometimes through no fault of their own," Melanie pointed out with feeling.

"A volunteer who comes to *them* wants to see them and the whole atmosphere between doctor and patient is different. The patients *trust* the doctor which in turn helps him treat them effectively," Melanie concluded.

Donnelly blew out a skeptical breath. "And this is your story," the woman asked Mitch.

Mitch never wavered. Instead, he met her gaze head on. "Quite honestly, it wasn't before, but it is now. Ms. McAdams has made me remember the real reason why I became a doctor in the first place."

He'd spent enough time waltzing around with this irritating woman, Mitch thought. He got down to the crux of the reason he'd come to the chapel. To back Melanie up any way he could.

"Now, I understand that there is a problem about her taking custody of April once the little girl is released from the hospital—which won't be for at least several days if not longer," he emphasized. "She sustained a number of serious internal injuries. Frankly," he interjected because he saw this as being of tantamount importance in this custody case that was erupting, "we thought we lost her. She stopped breathing at the scene of the accident. It was Ms. McAdams who refused to give up on her even when April's heart stopped beating. She continued holding on to April, pleading with her to come back to us. I had almost managed to get Ms. McAdams to let go of her when April opened her eyes."

Donnelly's skepticism mushroomed. "Ah, so perhaps I should add Miracle Worker to Ms. McAdams's résumé," she said, her voice dripping with sarcasm.

Mitch's expression never changed. Remaining stony, it was almost unnerving. Melanie could see Donnelly eyeing him nervously.

"I think that most of us would agree that faith, no matter how clichéd it sounds, works in mysterious ways," Mitch said. "I know it was an eye-opener for me. Now, I can give you a written recommendation for Ms. McAdams in order to make this custody thing happen. I can also get you a statement, if necessary, from the chief administrator of this hospital." When Donnelly made no response, he went on to say, "I also know several heads of—"

Donnelly held up a hand as if in mute surrender. "Not necessary," the social worker told him. "Your statement is more than sufficient, Doctor." She glanced at Melanie, obvious less than happy about the fact that she had to concede the battle to her. As a parting shot, Donnelly said, "It might help matters if Ms. McAdams was married, but—"

"That is in the offing, as well," Mitch told her in a quiet, serious voice, cutting her off.

It took considerable concentrated effort on Melanie's part to keep her jaw from dropping. She had to remind herself that Mitch was saying a great many things right now just to make the woman back off and go away and for that she would be eternally grateful.

Jennifer Donnelly was a bulldog when she needed to be, but she also knew when she was outgunned and defeated. And she was now.

"I'll get to the paperwork right away." Donnelly put her hand out to Melanie. It wasn't a heartfelt gesture, but it was as genuine as she could manage. "Congratulations, Ms. McAdams. A lot of paperwork has to be finalized but it looks like you have yourself a little girl." The smile that followed the statement could be called nothing short of spasmodic.

"Thank you," Melanie answered with relief and enthusiasm. "I'll take excellent care of her. This *is* for her best interests."

Donnelly couldn't resist one final sniff. "So I am told," she said, looking directly at Mitch. "I'll be back with the papers in the morning."

"I'll be here," Melanie assured her. The moment the woman had left the chapel, she turned to Mitch. "Do you actually *know* all those people you just offered to get letters from?"

There was no change in his expression. "I do."

Okay, maybe he did, but that still didn't touch the important issue. "But they wouldn't go as far as give me a statement of recommendation—"

"They would," he told her without fanfare. "They don't like bureaucracy any better than I do. And if their letters failed to do the trick, I could always sic my mother on that woman. *That* would definitely do it. My mother is one gutsy little lady." A smile curved the corners of his mouth as he looked at Melanie. "Kind of like someone else I know," he told her.

"Thank you," Melanie said, suddenly choking up. Tears were coming at an unstoppable rate, sliding down her cheeks and threatening to go on indefinitely.

Sitting back down in the pew, Mitch took her into his arms and held her until she could regain control of herself.

"No," he told her quietly when her tears finally subsided, "Thank *you*. I meant what I said. If it wasn't for you, I wouldn't have been volunteering at the shelter, which means I wouldn't have been there in time to save April—and even then, if not for you, April would have been lost. You opened my eyes to a great many things," he told her.

Melanie wiped her eyes and did what she could to pull herself together. She glanced in the direction that the social worker had taken.

"She'll be back, you know," she said. "In the morning, like she said."

"I know," he told her. "I never doubted it for a moment. Her kind always is. But I'll be here to back you up, just like I said. In writing, in spirit, in any way you need. If she wants letters of recommendation, she'll get them." And then he had a question for her. "You know for a fact that you have that job waiting for you at your old school?"

Melanie nodded. "Absolutely. The principal still calls me on occasion to check in and see how I'm doing. I spoke to her about a week and a half ago, told her I was slowly getting there."

Taking it in, Mitch nodded. "Good, although not entirely necessary," he went on to tell her. When she looked at him quizzically, he explained, "The factor here as far as Social Services is concerned is money—"

Melanie thought she knew what he was about to say. "No," she told him firmly.

His brow furrowed. "No?"

Melanie backtracked, knowing she'd jumped the gun but fairly confident she hadn't guessed wrong. "If you're about to tell me you'll lend me whatever money you think they want in my bank account, the answer's no. I won't take any money from you."

Mitch's expression was unreadable as he murmured, "I see."

"You've done too much for me already," Melanie insisted. "You saved April—twice," she emphasized. "Once right after the accident and just now." As far as she was concerned, that was twice he'd brought the little girl back to her. "I can never repay you for either time, but that doesn't mean I'm not going to really try." She went on to explain her reasoning. "Borrowing money from you would only make the debt that much more huge," she told him.

"Are you finished?" Mitch asked mildly when she finally paused for breath and stopped talking for a moment.

Melanie inclined her head. "Yes."

He looked into her eyes, as if expecting to find his answer there. "You're sure?"

"Yes." Impatience rimmed itself around the single word.

"Okay, because I wasn't going to offer to lend you money—" Mitch started to tell her. He didn't get any further.

"I won't *take* any from you, either," she said with feeling, guessing that he was going to just make it a matter of semantics.

He gave her what she thought was a reproving look, the kind a teacher would give a particularly trying student after being tested yet again. "I thought you said you were finished."

"Okay. Yes, *now* I'm finished," she told him. Melanie saw him looking at her as if he was waiting for her to add a PS to her statement. "Totally," she added by way of a closing. Since he was still waiting for a better sign, she crossed her heart to seal the deal.

"Satisfied?" she asked.

His nod was her answer. "All right. I wasn't going to offer to lend—or *give*—you money," Mitch told her, his tone quiet, subdued. "What I was going to do was ask you to marry me."

Melanie was utterly and completely stunned, not to mention speechless.

Chapter Sixteen

"Not right now," Mitch quickly qualified when Melanie said nothing. He didn't want her to think that he was in any way rushing her. "I mean, I'm asking you now, but I'm not asking you to marry me now."

He saw confusion slipping over her features. He found himself *really* wishing he had better communication skills.

"Not coming out very well, I know, but then, I never exactly pictured myself being in this position, either. Asking someone to marry me," he specified. "I was fine just the way I was. Or, at least I *thought* I was fine just the way I was," Mitch added. "What I'm asking you to do is *think* about marrying me. Doesn't have to be today, next week or even next month. I just want you to *think* about the idea.

"I won't lie to you, I've been trying to talk myself

out of this ever since I first experienced this strange, overwhelming feeling. I thought it was my imagination, or just the result of being on overload, a by-product of the marathon stressful situation I found myself under—double shifts, volunteer work," he went on to explain. "But the more I tried to tell myself this, this *excuse*, the more I realized that I was just rationalizing, and doing a damn bad job of it."

He smiled at her, wondering how he'd gotten so lucky without even trying. "I realized that I was actually *feeling* what some people spend their whole lives chasing after and never feeling. I love you," he told her in case there was some confusion about what he meant. "And now, I need to know how you feel." He summoned his courage and put it all on the line. For perhaps the first time in his life, he was scared, scared he wouldn't hear what he desperately needed to hear. "I need to know if you love me."

Melanie pressed her lips together, struggling to keep her tears back. Crying would only add to the stress here. "I don't want to love you."

Mitch nodded, but that wasn't what he had asked. "I get that." He understood, or thought he did, the depth of her fear, the sheer terror of being afraid of having her heart ripped out again because someone she loved was taken from her. Which made her love all the more precious if she could just risk it. Risk it for him. "But do you?"

"Yes," she admitted quietly, looking down at the floor. She tried to turn away, but he gently placed his hands on her shoulders and forced Melanie to look up at him.

He looked into her eyes, confident that he would

see the truth no matter what she actually tried to say, or tell him.

"You love me." It was half a question, half a hopeful statement.

She closed her eyes and sighed, as if saying the words out loud were hurtful to her, as well as setting her up for an entire ocean of pain down the line.

"Yes."

"Open your eyes and look at me, Melanie. Please," he added when she was slow to comply. Melanie opened her eyes. They looked right into his. "Now say it."

"Yes."

He needed to hear the entire sentence. Desperate to be convinced, he needed it all. "Yes what?"

"Yes, I love you." The words were accompanied by fresh tears. The admission was actually painful. "Satisfied?"

"It's not a matter of being satisfied, Melanie. It's a matter of needing to know if I'm forcing you into something or if you really mean it on your own." What he saw in her eyes at that moment gave him his answer. "You do."

"Yes," she told him in a choked whisper, "and I'm scared to death."

Oh damn, her tears were going to be his undoing. "I don't want you to cry—"

Melanie struggled to smile through the tears. "Sorry, comes with the territory, can't have one without the other."

"Duly noted," he told her, taking her back into his arms. Then, very gently, he raised her chin until she was looking up at him and then he kissed her. Softly, as if her lips were rose petals and if he pressed too hard, they were liable to be crushed and drift down to the floor.

"I can't make you promises that are beyond my power to keep," Mitch told her honestly. "I can't tell you that I'm going to live forever, although I certainly am going to try," he added with a fond smile. "What I *can* promise is that for as long as I *do* live, I will love you and do everything in my power for you to never even have one moment's regret for loving me."

That much *was* in his power to promise her.

"Can't ask for more than that," she replied in a voice so low that it was almost a whisper.

And then, taking another breath, she knew there was something that they *hadn't* really talked about yet. Not as far as it related to the situation he had just painted for the two of them.

"You do realize that I come as a set," Melanie said, broaching the subject carefully.

Having said it out loud, she knew and readily accepted the fact that she loved this man who had come so unexpectedly into her life. But she didn't have just herself to think of anymore.

Mitch tilted his head a little, as if trying to absorb what she had just alluded to.

"I *am* going to adopt April," she told him.

Why did she feel she had to tell him this, he wondered. "I know. I just made it easier for you, remember?"

"That's not going to change your mind?" she asked. "Taking on a wife *and* a child?" she stressed to make sure he got the full impact of his proposal. "That's a ready-made family and there're going to be a lot of adjustments needing to be made—on everyone's part."

"I'm aware of that," then added tongue-in-cheek although he kept a straight face, "I took psychology as part of my doctor training."

"That's a pretty brave move for a man who is 'just fine' being alone."

He knew he should have put that part better, Mitch thought, but it was too late to go back and begin again. "Let's just say I was in a cave all this time and now that I've 'stepped out into the light,' I want it all—the light, the warmth, the whole nine yards. Make that twelve yards."

"Twelve?" She didn't understand the reference.

He grinned and she found him appealingly boyish-looking when he did that. "I was always an over-achiever," Mitch told her.

She felt like laughing and crying at the same time. It took everything Melanie had not to throw her arms around his neck.

"We need to run this by April," she told him. "I know she loves you, but I want her to be prepared for all the changes that are going to be coming."

"Understood." How could one woman be so warm and loving and yet so incredibly organized, he couldn't help wondering in complete admiration. "I really doubt she's going to have any objections, not the way she hung on to you," he reminded her.

"And your mother," Melanie suddenly said, thinking out loud.

Mitch looked at her, puzzled. What was she talking about?

"April didn't hang on to my mother," he told her.

Melanie shook her head. Her tongue was getting all tangled. "No, I mean you're going to want to run this by your mother, aren't you? I mean, she doesn't even know I exist." The more she talked, the more nervous she grew at the idea of facing this hurdle. "This is some bombshell you're going to be dropping on her. A lot of mothers are kind of possessive when it comes to their sons," she told him.

She'd seen it time and again at the shelter. More than a few single mothers there *were* single mothers because of this exact problem. The men they were with had mothers who squelched the entire union between their son and the women they had created families with.

Mitch laughed. "My mother is going to be even more on board with this than April. There'll probably be fireworks."

"Fireworks?" Melanie repeated nervously.

Was he saying that his mother was going to read him the riot act over this? Or blow up when he told her? The last thing she wanted was to come between Mitch and *anyone*, least of all his mother.

"As in the kind they use on the Fourth of July to celebrate," he elaborated. "Skywriting will probably be involved, as well."

Melanie could only stare at him. What was he talking about? "Skywriting?"

"As in, My Prayers Have Been Answered. He's Finally Getting Married!" Laughing, Mitch kissed her fleetingly, but nonetheless with feeling. "Trust me, she wasn't the type to nag, but my mother has been waiting a very long time for this. All of her friends' children have already made them grandmothers."

Now that it was behind him, he could laugh as he re-called certain scenarios. "She got very creative with dropping hints indirectly." His mother, he thought, was going to *love* Melanie. "Now I guess the only thing left is to decide when."

"When we'll get married?" she asked, guessing at the rest of his sentence.

That was getting ahead of the game. "No, when you'll answer me."

Melanie's eyebrows narrowed as she tried to under-stand what he was saying. "I'm not sure I follow—"

"You haven't given me your answer and I prom-ised not to pressure you, so after we go see April to tell her that she'll be coming home with us—with you for the time being," Mitch corrected himself, "when she's discharged from the hospital, then the next order of business will be—"

"Yes," she interjected almost breathlessly. It felt good to say the word, she couldn't help thinking. Ev-erything felt right about this.

Stopping abruptly in his narrative, Mitch looked at her. "Excuse me?"

Melanie smiled broadly and repeated. "Yes."

He was afraid to allow himself to believe this could be so easy. There was something he was overlook-ing. "Yes, what?"

"Yes," she told him, enunciating each word slowly, "I'll marry you."

"I said I didn't want to pressure you," he reminded her. Even so, the sound of her acceptance caused his heart rate to accelerate.

"I know. And I said yes. You're not pressuring me, Mitch," she assured him. "If anything, *I've* been pressuring me. Pressuring me *not* to set myself up so that I would ever possibly be in that awful position to feel that kind of pain again. But ultimately that means not feeling at all and you know, not feeling is just as bad as feeling too much."

He smiled at her. "Tell me about it," he thought, remembering how he'd been such a short while ago.

"Besides, I'm already in that position," she admitted. "I love April to pieces and the thought of that little girl being forced to live somewhere else just because some autonomous department felt it was for 'her own good,' the thought of her being frightened and lonely and possibly who knows what, well, that was already ripping out my heart—so what's a little more added fear in that mix?" she asked.

"What indeed," Mitch agreed, giving in and kissing her again. This time, it took more of an effort to get himself to stop than it had just previously. "We'd better get out of here," he told her, rising in the pew and taking her hand. "Otherwise, if we stick around here any longer like this, I might just forget I have a reputation to maintain."

Melanie looked at him in surprise, although she would have been lying if she'd said that what he'd just admitted shocked her. Part of her was feeling the same thing, even though she pointed out the obvious deterrent. "We're in a chapel."

"We're alone," he countered which, right now, seemed more to the point to him than *where* they were.

Drawing her out into the hall, he said, "C'mon, let's go see April and give her the good news."

But then a slight bit of hesitation came over him.

It was a feeling he was definitely unfamiliar with—as unfamiliar as what he experienced each and every time he was around Melanie these days, or even just *thought* of Melanie these days.

"She will see that as good news, won't she?" he asked Melanie. "I don't mean her being with you, but her getting me in the bargain as her dad."

Rather than try to convince him, Melanie simply took his hand and said, "Let's ask her."

"Best news ever!" the little girl declared less than ten minutes later.

They'd found her in her room, awake and struggling not just to sit up, but to get out of bed. Apparently she hadn't really been asleep when Jennifer Donnelly had made her intentions clear to the nurse who was there watching over her—the nurse who then called Mitch to alert him as to what was going on.

Afraid that she would be taken away at any moment, April was trying to get up and get dressed so she could make good her escape before the social worker came back to her room.

"No, honey, no," Melanie had assured her once April had blurted out why she was trying to get away. Very gently she'd pressed April back into her hospital bed. "No one is taking you anywhere, especially since you're not well enough to leave the hospital for a few days yet."

"But then that lady with the big voice is going to come get me and I don't wanna go with her," April had cried, big tears sliding down her small face. "I want to be with you." She'd looked at Melanie as she'd said it. Melanie had felt her heart twisting in her chest for what April had been going through.

"No, she won't. Dr. Mitch saw to that," Melanie had told her. "He won't let her take you." She'd taken April's hand in hers before continuing. "April, how would you like to come live with me and be my little girl?"

"I could do that?" April had asked, her eyes wide with surprise.

"Most definitely. I'd like to adopt you so that nobody can ever take you away from me again." She looked down into the little girl's open face, thinking how much she loved her. It didn't seem possible to love someone so much so quickly, and yet she did. Twice over, she thought, glancing toward Mitch. She had looked back at April and asked, "Would that be okay with you?"

"Yes!" April had cried, looking happy enough to burst.

"There's more," Melanie had went on, choosing her words carefully. "Dr. Mitch asked me to marry him."

"What did you say?" April had asked, looking not at her but at Mitch.

"I said yes," Melanie told her.

Instead of looking happy, April's face had become pensive. It had been obvious that she was trying to sort some things out. "So that means you *won't* adopt me?" she'd asked, confused.

"No, that means I—we both want to ask you how you feel about something," Melanie began.

Impatient, Mitch cut in. "How would you feel about me becoming your dad?" he asked April, unable to stay silent and remain in the background any longer, not when something was this important.

And that was when the little girl had cried, "Best news ever! I mean, I wish Mama and Jimmy were here," she added quickly, "but if they can't be, I'm sure glad that you are. We're gonna be a family?" she asked excitedly, looking from Melanie to Mitch and then back again, unable to contain her enthusiasm.

"Yes, we are," Mitch told her. Everything felt right he thought. For the first time, everything felt as if it had fallen into place just where it belonged.

"Does this mean you'll hug and kiss, too?" April asked out of the blue. "Mama said that when Daddy was alive, he used to hug and kiss her all the time. She said that was what she missed about him the most. That was why I used to hug and kiss her a lot, so she wouldn't miss Daddy so much. But if Dr. Mitch is gonna be my daddy," she went on in that innocently wise way that some children had, "that means he can hug and kiss you, right? I like hugging and kissing," she told them, her voice growing smaller, "but I'm tired right now so if you need a hug," she said to Melanie, then turned toward Mitch, "can you do it for me?"

"I think I can manage that, yes," Mitch told April, doing his best not to laugh. "As a matter of fact, I can give you a little demonstration right now."

"Okay," April told him.

It was the last word she said before her eyelids, already heavy, closed and she fell asleep.

Mitch didn't notice.

He was too busy fulfilling his new daughter's request and hugging Melanie. He threw the kissing in for good measure.

There were no complaints from Melanie.

Epilogue

"Well, ladies, one more for our plus column," Theresa Manetti whispered to her friends as she slid into the last pew of the Bedford Rescue Mission's chapel, taking a seat beside Maizie and Celia Parnell.

Theresa had just finished checking—again—on the meal she had prepared and was catering for Mitch and Melanie's wedding reception. She joined Maizie, who had just gotten into the pew a couple of minutes ahead of her, having given a final hearty congratulations to the groom's mother, an utterly thrilled, and grateful, Charlotte Stewart.

The wedding, at both the bride *and* the groom's insistence, was taking place here, at the Bedford Rescue Mission where they had first met and become, with the recently finalized addition of April, a family.

It was difficult to say who among the guests, and this included Polly, the shelter's director, was the most thrilled about the union: the guests, the director, the groom's mother, their newly adopted daughter, or the two main participants of the ceremony. From all indications, it appeared to be a multi-way tie.

Celia leaned in toward her friends, keeping her voice extra low so that only they heard her. "That worries me," she confided.

The other two exchanged glances before looking in unison at their friend. Although thought to be the more thoughtful and somber of the trio, Celia wasn't exactly anyone's idea of a pessimist.

"How so?" Maizie asked.

Celia was not happy about the reason she offered. "Well, so far, we're batting a thousand, agreed?"

"That's what it's called when there's a hundred percent success, yes, dear," Maizie confirmed indulgently.

And, as amazing as it might seem to the outside observer, every single one of the couples they had stealthily brought together using dozens of pretexts had not only hit it off, but had gotten married and were *still* happily married.

Celia hesitated, searching for the right words. "Well, don't you think that's kind of like, tempting fate?"

"Tempting fate to do what, exactly?" Theresa wanted to know. She was still unclear about their friend's reasoning.

"Tempting fate to have our efforts fall short and fail," Celia finally said, looking less than happy about putting her feelings into actual words.

Maizie looked totally unfazed by Celia's theory. "I don't know, I'd rather say that it puts the odds in our favor."

"Yes, but—" Celia began.

But Maizie waved the woman beside her into silence—at least for now.

The opening strains of the wedding march had begun to swell through the mission's chapel and as the rear entrance doors parted, April, fully recovered and dressed in a frilly pink dress Melanie had let her pick out herself, was doing her version of a two-step, proudly strewing pink rose petals from the open basket that was slung over her small forearm.

There was a huge pink bow on the basket and a smaller one jauntily tied in her hair.

A moment later Melanie entered on the arm of Theresa's son. The latter had offered to give the bride away since own her father was deceased.

"What a beautiful bride," Celia sighed.

"Each one of them looks more beautiful than the last," Theresa whispered as tears began to slide through her lashes.

"As it should be," Maizie murmured to her friends. "As it should be."

"Shhh," Celia warned, not wanting their voices to carry and distract the bride as she walked by.

There seemed to be little danger of that. Melanie only had eyes for the man standing tall and proud at the front of the altar. The man for whom her heart had broken all of her rules.

Dr. Mitchell Stewart, her second chance at love and happily-ever-after.

Blowing a kiss to April, who was watching her intently from the sidelines now, Melanie took her place beside Mitch, a place from which she planned to face the rest of her life.

* * * * *

COMING NEXT MONTH FROM

HARLEQUIN®

SPECIAL EDITION

Available February 16, 2016

#2461 "I DO"...TAKE TWO!
Three Coins in the Fountain
by Merline Lovelace
On a trip to Italy, Kate Westbrook makes a wish at the Trevi Fountain—to create a future *without* her soon-to-be-ex, Travis! But Cupid has other plans for these two, and true love might just be in their future.

#2462 FORTUNE'S SECRET HUSBAND
The Fortunes of Texas: All Fortune's Children
by Karen Rose Smith
Proper Brit Lucie Fortune Chesterfield had a whirlwind teenage marriage to Chase Parker, but that was long over—or so she thought. Until her secret husband shows up at her door...with a big surprise!

#2463 BACK IN THE SADDLE
Wed in the West
by Karen Templeton
When widower Zach Talbot agrees to help Mallory Keyes find a horse for her son, he falls for the paralyzed former actress. But can the veterinarian and the beauty both give love a second chance?

#2464 A BABY AND A BETROTHAL
Crimson, Colorado
by Michelle Major
Katie Garrity is on a mission to find her perfect match—only to be surprised by her own pregnancy! When her first crush, Noah Crawford, comes back to town, will they get a chance at a love neither expected?

#2465 FROM DARE TO DUE DATE
Sugar Falls, Idaho
by Christy Jeffries
When dancer Mia Palinski has one magical night with Dr. Garrett McCormick, she winds up pregnant. Both of them aren't looking for love, but a baby changes everything. Can a single dance create a forever family?

#2466 A COWBOY IN THE KITCHEN
Hurley's Homestyle Kitchen
by Meg Maxwell
Single dad West Montgomery is doing his best to be Mr. Mom for his daughter. He's even taking cooking classes with beautiful chef Annabel Hurley. But West and his little girl might be the secret ingredient for her perfect recipe to forever.

YOU CAN FIND MORE INFORMATION ON UPCOMING HARLEQUIN® TITLES, FREE EXCERPTS AND MORE AT WWW.HARLEQUIN.COM.

HSECNM0216

REQUEST YOUR FREE BOOKS!

2 FREE NOVELS PLUS 2 FREE GIFTS!

♦ HARLEQUIN®

SPECIAL EDITION

Life, Love & Family

YES! Please send me 2 FREE Harlequin® Special Edition novels and my 2 FREE gifts (gifts are worth about $10). After receiving them, if I don't wish to receive any more books, I can return the shipping statement marked "cancel." If I don't cancel, I will receive 6 brand-new novels every month and be billed just $4.74 per book in the U.S. or $5.49 per book in Canada. That's a savings of at least 12% off the cover price! It's quite a bargain! Shipping and handling is just 50¢ per book in the U.S. and 75¢ per book in Canada.* I understand that accepting the 2 free books and gifts places me under no obligation to buy anything. I can always return a shipment and cancel at any time. Even if I never buy another book, the two free books and gifts are mine to keep forever.

235/335 HDN GH3Z

Name	(PLEASE PRINT)

Address	Apt. #

City	State/Prov.	Zip/Postal Code

Signature (if under 18, a parent or guardian must sign)

Mail to the **Reader Service:**
IN U.S.A.: P.O. Box 1867, Buffalo, NY 14240-1867
IN CANADA: P.O. Box 609, Fort Erie, Ontario L2A 5X3

Want to try two free books from another line?
Call 1-800-873-8635 or visit www.ReaderService.com.

* Terms and prices subject to change without notice. Prices do not include applicable taxes. Sales tax applicable in N.Y. Canadian residents will be charged applicable taxes. Offer not valid in Quebec. This offer is limited to one order per household. Not valid for current subscribers to Harlequin Special Edition books. All orders subject to credit approval. Credit or debit balances in a customer's account(s) may be offset by any other outstanding balance owed by or to the customer. Please allow 4 to 6 weeks for delivery. Offer available while quantities last.

Your Privacy—The Reader Service is committed to protecting your privacy. Our Privacy Policy is available online at www.ReaderService.com or upon request from the Reader Service.

We make a portion of our mailing list available to reputable third parties that offer products we believe may interest you. If you prefer that we not exchange your name with third parties, or if you wish to clarify or modify your communication preferences, please visit us at www.ReaderService.com/consumerschoice or write to us at Reader Service Preference Service, P.O. Box 9062, Buffalo, NY 14240-9062. Include your complete name and address.

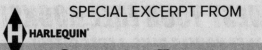

SPECIAL EXCERPT FROM

HARLEQUIN

SPECIAL EDITION

All Kate Westbrook wants to do on her trip to Italy is to get over her soon-to-be ex-husband. But then irresistible Air Force pilot Travis shows up in Rome! When Travis offers to whisk her off for one last adventure, can Kate resist the man who still holds the key to her heart?

Read on for a sneak preview of
"I DO"...TAKE TWO!
by *Merline Lovelace,*
the first book in her new miniseries,
THREE COINS IN THE FOUNTAIN.

Travis had heard the words come out of his mouth and been as stunned as the two men he'd come to know so well in recent weeks. Yet as soon as his brain had processed the audio signals, he'd recognized their unshakable truth. If trading his Air Force flight suit for one with an EAS patch on it would win Kate back, he'd make the change today.

"So what do you think?" he asked her. "Again, your first no-frills, no-holds-barred gut reaction?"

"I won't lie," she admitted slowly, reluctantly. "My head, my heart, my gut all leaped for joy."

He started for her, elation pumping through his veins. The hand she slapped against his chest to stop him made only a tiny dent in his fierce joy.

"Wait, Trav! This is too big a decision to make without talking it over. Let's…let's use this time together to make sure it's what you really want."

"I'm sure. Now."

"Well, I'm not." Her brown eyes showed an agony of doubt. "The military's been your whole life up to now."

"Wrong." He laid his hand over hers, felt the warmth of her palm against his sternum. "You came first, Katydid. Before the uniform, before the wings, before the head rush and stomach-twisting responsibilities of being part of a crew. I let those get in the way the past few years. That won't happen again."

The doubt was still there in her eyes, swimming in a pool of indecision. He needed to back off, Travis conceded. Give her a few days to accept what was now a done deal in his mind.

"Okay," he said with a sense of rightness he hadn't felt in longer than he could remember, "we'll head up to Venice. Let Ellis's proposal percolate for a day or two."

And then, he vowed, they would conduct a virtual burning of the divorce decree before he took his wife to bed.

Don't miss
"I DO"…TAKE TWO!
by USA TODAY bestselling author Merline Lovelace,
available March 2016 wherever
Harlequin® Special Edition books and ebooks are sold.

www.Harlequin.com

Love the Harlequin book you just read?

Your opinion matters.

Review this book on your favorite book site, review site, blog or your own social media properties and share your opinion with other readers!

Be sure to connect with us at:
Harlequin.com/Newsletters
Facebook.com/HarlequinBooks
Twitter.com/HarlequinBooks